A DICTATOR CALLS

A DICTATOR CALLS

A novel

ISMAIL KADARE

TRANSLATED FROM THE ALBANIAN BY
JOHN HODGSON

COUNTERPOINT

Berkeley, California

A DICTATOR CALLS

This is a work of fiction. All of the characters, organizations, and events portrayed in this novel are either products of the author's imagination or are used fictitiously.

Copyright © 2022, Librairie Arthème Fayard
All rights reserved.
Translation copyright © 2023 by John Hodsgon

All rights reserved under domestic and international copyright. Outside of fair use (such as quoting within a book review), no part of this publication may be reproduced, stored in a retrieval system, or transmitted in any form or by any means, electronic, mechanical, photocopying, recording, or otherwise, without the written permission of the publisher. For permissions, please contact the publisher.

First Counterpoint paperback edition: 2023

Library of Congress Cataloging-in-Publication Data
Names: Kadare, Ismail, author. | Hodgson, John, 1951– translator.
Title: A dictator calls : a novel / Ismail Kadare ; translated from the Albanian by John Hodgson.
Other titles: Kur sunduesit grinden. English
Description: Berkeley, California : Counterpoint, 2023.
Identifiers: LCCN 2023019021 | ISBN 9781640096080 (trade paperback) | ISBN 9781640096097 (ebook)
Subjects: LCSH: Stalin, Joseph, 1878–1953—Fiction. | Pasternak, Boris Leonidovich, 1890–1960—Fiction. | LCGFT: Historical fiction. | Novels.
Classification: LCC PG9621.K3 K8613 2023 | DDC 891/.9913—dc23/eng/20230501
LC record available at https://lccn.loc.gov/2023019021

Cover design and illustration by Farjana Yasmin

COUNTERPOINT
2560 Ninth Street, Suite 318
Berkeley, CA 94710
www.counterpointpress.com

Printed in the United States of America

1 3 5 7 9 10 8 6 4 2

A DICTATOR CALLS

PART
ONE

THE STOP is on the right-hand side of the street. Trolleybus number three. Take it as far as Pushkin Square. That's where the statue is, as you no doubt know. *Exegi monumentum*, etc. Walk past, with the statue on your right, cross Gorky Street, and Tverskoi Boulevard begins at the crossroads a few steps further on.

Then everything is straightforward. After a minute's walk, the gate of the Gorky Institute appears on your right. It's obvious, you understand. Even if you don't want to see this monument, there it is . . . Why shouldn't I want to see it? Who knows. Whenever we think that we want something, in fact we don't.

No, I've made such an effort to get this far. The trolleybuses whinny like wild horses. Potholes everywhere. Then at last I glimpse the famous statue. Walk past, with the statue on your right, they'd said.

'What statue, young man? You're talking

nonsense. There are no statues like that around here . . . What do you mean?'

'The statue of Pushkin. I walked past it so often.'

'Your eyes deceived you. There's never been anything like that here.'

'But everyone in the world knows about it: *exegi monumentum . . .*'

'As you said, I raised a monument not made by human hands – a *nerukotvorniy* monument. You fell into the trap yourself. A monument raised not by human hands, but by the spirit, as the poet says. A statue that nobody can see, apart from the insane, like you students at the Gorky Institute.'

'We weren't insane.'

'You were worse. Each of you dreamed of toppling each other's statue, in order to raise your own.'

'Like the Pasternak rally? No, that was different.'

4

'Were you at that rally? Did you howl against him?'

'Never.'

'Then what did you do while the others howled?'

'I looked at a girl in tears. I thought she was his niece.'

'And you've come back, after so many years, to see this place again? Does it seem to you that the rally is still going on?'

'Perhaps. In fact, it probably is. You can pinpoint the assembly point from the distant shouts, more easily than from the sign by the Institute's gate. It's the same incessant noise in Moscow as one hears in Tirana.'

This nightmare came back again and again for years, in the most bizarre forms. The groaning of the trolleybuses over the bumps and potholes in the street. The monument under threat. The tears, and sweet Moscow.

I was so sure I would write about it that at times it was as if I'd already done so, or that the supply of words I needed was ready and waiting, stockpiled in the proper corner.

The ever more frequent dream journeys were a sure sign that the time was ripe. The dreams became more confused and illogical. Trolleybus number three refused to set off, and they had to strike it with a whip. How long had this been going on? Many things had changed in the years since I'd left Moscow, but surely they hadn't got to the point of whipping trolleybuses.

In Tirana the official campaign for the arts to get to grips with life continued. Writers, almost without exception, admitted to falling short, especially when it came to comprehending the lives of workers in factories, let alone on cooperative farms. Meanwhile, without telling anybody, I'd started my novel about Moscow, but I wasn't at all sure that I'd get to the end, just as Moscow itself was now out of reach. After the breakdown of diplomatic relations, there was no hope of taking a trip there. I would fall asleep and long to find myself back once more. But I felt that less and less often. Moreover, in my dreams the chaos of the city grew more intense, and I couldn't tell whether this chaos was an obstacle or was helping me in what I wanted to do.

As it turned out, it helped me, and in contrast to the realities of factories and farms, Moscow required a sense of distance.

In one of the dreams, after I'd crossed Pushkin Square almost on my knees, I found most of the students at the rally. I knew that my own name would be on the placards, but still I was surprised to see it. Then, increasingly clearly, I heard the shouting against me.

Among the students were several of my friends from the Gorky Institute. Petros Anteos didn't know where to look, while Stulpans, a Latvian and my closest friend, held his head in his hands.

'The big boss in Tirana telephoned you,'

shouted an angry Belorussian. 'That Stalin of yours, I've forgotten his name.'

I nodded in confirmation, but he didn't calm down.

How many versions of the telephone call are there?

I couldn't remember. I wanted to tell him probably three or four, no more. But I didn't manage to because I woke up.

Enver Hoxha's phone call had indeed taken place some time before this dream. It was midday, and I was at the Writers' Union as usual when the deputy chief editor of the newspaper *Drita* held out the receiver and said that someone was asking for me.

'I am Haxhi Kroi,' the voice said. 'Comrade Enver wants to speak with you.'

I didn't manage to say anything, except 'thank you'! The leader congratulated me on a poem that had been recently published in the newspaper. I said 'thank you' again. He said that he'd liked it a lot. I signalled to the people round me to keep quiet, but I was in no state to say anything else apart from a third 'thank you'.

'What are all these thank-yous, one after another?' asked one of the editors. 'Since when so polite?'

I didn't know how to warn him, so I merely made another ambiguous hand signal.

'That was Enver Hoxha.' Those were the only words I managed to utter after the call ended.

'Really? How come? The man himself?'

'Yes,' I replied.

'What for? What did he say to you, and you – why didn't you say anything?'

I said I didn't know. I'd been taken aback.

I told him about the congratulations, and he said again what a shame it was I hadn't replied properly. But someone else said I had done all right, and that moments like that leave you tongue-tied.

I spoke to the Belorussian in my dream. 'Idiot,' I said.

During the campaign against his reputation, Pasternak's phone conversation with Stalin was cited as one of the principal ways the poet had been shamed, especially the part where Stalin asked him what he thought of Mandelstam. There were five or six versions of the phone call in public circulation, but people spoke of many more, each worse than the last.

'Idiot,' I muttered, insulting the Belorussian again, but thinking more of myself, for conjuring such dreams.

Yet still I racked my brains, wondering if there could have been even more versions:

Comrade Enver wants to speak with you . . . What do you think of Mandelstam? That is of Lasgush Poradeci, or Pasko or Marko, who . . . prison. Although they have just come out of prison, they might go back . . . Or more simply, what about Agolli, Qiriazi, Arapi . . . who . . .

prison . . . although they haven't been to prison yet. Or to get to the point, what do you think of yourself?

I would have found this last question about myself easier than the others. Like everyone else, my intention was to write about real life . . . apart from an unpublished novella, which might have caused Comrade X a problem if it came to his attention, about student life in Moscow, although most of the events take place far away in a writers' holiday home at a place called Dubulti on the Baltic coast.

What is your opinion of Pasternak?

This question felt surprising, although it was nothing of the sort. In truth, it was the one question I didn't want to be asked.

Pasternak? I never had anything to do with him. Except one day I saw him from a distance in Peredelkino. And if he's mentioned in the course of the novella, this is in connection with the campaign against him, part of the background against which the events take place. There was a relative of his at the Gorky Institute, a woman in the second year, whose eyes were always full of tears, for reasons that can be imagined.

I was ready to go into unnecessary detail, if only to avoid the next question, which seemed to me even worse, about the Nobel Prize.

Most of the students, as they howled in chorus to denounce the prize, dreamed of nothing else but winning it. However, the question wasn't about them, but about myself. Should I say that the Nobel Prize had never crossed my mind? Of course not. I'd thought of it often, but especially years later when it was whispered that I myself . . . might be on that list.

So to me this uproar against Pasternak included a strange and entirely different element. As if it were not only about him but about someone else, perhaps even myself. This produced in me a severe but intoxicating anxiety. Imagine standing alone in front of your country, which insults you and yells in your face with hatred and love at the same time. Give back that cursed prize, scream the students, pregnant women, the miners of Tepelenë. But you, a capricious waverer, like Hamlet in his dilemma, can't decide whether to take it or not to take it. Then the father of literature Sterjo Spasse, just in the way that Korney Chukovsky visited Pasternak in his dacha, comes to you and says, you are like a son to me, I'm here today, but I'll be gone tomorrow, for the sake of your memories of Moscow, turn down that poisoned chalice before it's too late!

Fortunately, I rarely found myself in this kind of state. What in my own mind I called my nocturnal Muscovite wanderings became less frequent once I started making notes for my novel. The only novel to take me more than ten years. Every now and then I would write a few pages and try to get stuck into it, or at least show I hadn't abandoned it.

It was like keeping a beautiful but highly dangerous bird in a cage. Sometimes you would get annoyed with it and, of course, with yourself. The irritation arose from the obligation that they (meaning the novel, I myself, some girls' hair, Moscow, art) had laid upon me to carry out that . . . rite. God knows for whom.

At other times, when I thought through the matter calmly, everything seemed more straightforward. I had no reason to dramatise the affair or complain to anybody, and still less to call this novel an obligation or . . . a rite. It was fuelled by my own incessant urge, which some people call a gift and others a madness or a demon. I separated the world into two parts, one part suitable for literature and the other not. The other was infinitely larger. But the suitable material came vaguely and in riddles, until one day, without analysing it thoroughly, I grasped hold of it.

Moscow became the part of the world that was suitable for literature at exactly the time when such a thing was no longer allowed. In place of the now impossible aircraft, visas and airports, there were only terrors of the night. The only remaining route to Moscow, which even the most terrifying tanks couldn't reach, was the novel.

It was no surprise that Moscow should become unavoidable at the very moment when the Soviet Union had become Tirana's enemy number one, but Pasternak's presence in this book was a surprise. What was he doing in the city which had just entered my own writing? With the girls' hair and the letters saying, 'You said you would come back.'

In short, could I write about these things without Pasternak? Each of us had his own writing to do. He with his serious worries, me with my devil-may-care student life.

The more I tried to persuade myself that leaving him out wouldn't be difficult, the harder it became, until I realised it was impossible. He'd been there . . . when everything happened. More precisely, I had been . . . there. I couldn't say he had nothing to do with me. We all had to deal with him, and always would, because we belonged to the same family, that of writers.

The question of family was a riddle that had been impenetrable to me in childhood. In reply to my persistent questions of why some people were our cousins and others not, my grandmother, after skirting the issue several times, had answered that God had said so, but that I shouldn't tell anyone.

What do you think of Mandelstam?

Boris Pasternak's reply, 'We're different, Comrade Stalin,' was often mentioned as proof that he had abandoned his friend.

The reply 'We're different' would come more easily to me, because we appeared so dissimilar: different nations, states, eras, religions too. Different languages, especially.

Yet we were family, and there was no changing this. Moscow became unavoidable from the day it became suitable for art, and our relationship through art made it impossible to avoid Pasternak.

Unable to avoid him, I would find myself caught in the middle between him and the communist state – either with the poet against the state or with the state against the poet. Or neutral, on neither side.

Incredibly, something had shifted: one could take sides against the Soviet state, but not the side of Pasternak. A hundred times no. From the Albanian point of view, the Soviet state had proved yet again that it was cruel, not because it had behaved badly towards the poet, but because it had treated him too gently.

One could imagine a meeting of the entire, as yet undivided socialist bloc, where a speaker would say, 'Comrades, states, republics, communist brothers, we are faced with a serious concern about one of our poets, who is the darling of the bourgeois world. Advise us on what we should do with him.' I was certain that two states, my own Albania and North Korea, would be the first to pipe up, 'What should we do? It's obvious. What we've always done: a bullet in the head, and the matter is closed.'

The situation had made it possible for me to adopt a previously unthinkable stance against the Soviet state. But the logical subsequent position of being pro-Pasternak was unimaginable.

Opposed to both. With one against the other. With both. With neither. All positions seemed crazy. The possibility of impartiality flickered and then died. I was a foreigner, and had found myself in this mess by chance. Let them do what they wanted, be reconciled or tear each other apart. It was nothing to do with me. I was different.

This train of thought merely issued in a ghastly

smile. In fact, I was not involved in this story by chance, but more mixed up in it than anyone else. It was beyond the question of family. There was a bond of terror between us. There in Peredelkino, on the ground floor of his dacha, lying on his narrow camp bed, Boris Pasternak was dying, killed by the Nobel Prize. In more than half a century since the prize was first given, the Russian poet was the first person it had killed. He would be mourned by his wife Zinaida Nikolayevna, and by his children, by strangers, and by his lover. It was May, I was still in Moscow, and I dimly sensed my future mysterious connection with him.

Years passed. Instead of this connection fading, the opposite happened. It became stronger than ever, and my denial couldn't break it.

For a time it wasn't clear to me whether it was the beautiful hair and eyes of the girls of Moscow that led me to Pasternak, or he that led me to them.

It was a story of impossibles: the impossibility of ever seeing again those eyes and that hair that I had filmed on my movie camera with such delight. But this was nothing compared to another vast and ominous impossibility. Our break with the socialist camp had fostered in us the illusion that sooner or later we would take our leave of socialism. Yet the signs indicated otherwise, and as time passed it became clearer that such a rupture was unlikely. The sad story of Pasternak was only one of many indicators that Moscow and Tirana were ready for a showdown, but as far as this accursed writer was concerned, their view and their policy were the same. Your reputation for good or ill is defined by our social-ist world, and as for that other world, forget it. Nothing but poison and grief comes from out there.

I had been published out there and no harm had come of it. This had happened to Pasternak too, before the scandal. Moscow had received the publication of *Doctor Zhivago* in silence, but if our stories had something in common, it was this initial silence. The second half, the uproar, was still to come.

I'd written a part of my novel about my Moscow years when the first rumours from Stockholm spread. This added mystery sometimes illuminated, sometimes shrouded the pages of my novel.

I had thought that these rumours would be enough to extinguish my desire to continue with the book. The proverb about not mentioning rope in the hanged man's house would provide sufficient reason. But that's not how it went. Nor did it turn out like that when my name first appeared in the list of nominees for the prize.

As if to put myself to a test, I took out my notes for the novel. I didn't take fright at them, but added something, with a hand that I thought would freeze at any moment. First a few lines, then whole pages. The threat of consequences if

I became famous abroad, and the feeling that we were all of us only prisoners on conditional release, seemed not to inhibit me.

I might remember everything from Moscow, even the women's hair and tears and breasts, which were so rare in Albanian literature, but it seemed impermissible to remember Pasternak. Being on the Nobel list meant being marked for danger like him. It was just my luck to undergo a similar fate, which in Pasternak's case death had cut short. Whether I wanted to be or not, I was an actor obliged to perform that role. So while it was natural for other people to ignore him, I couldn't. Yet other days came when the opposite seemed more logical, that anyone might talk about him except myself.

Then a third dimension appeared, that of literature, which resembled a dream in which worries and dangers fade away until they become like distant impersonal silhouettes.

In that third dimension I had done something

strange, irrelevant and totally incredible: I had finished my impossible novel.

My worries, which I liked to call nightmares, were deep down not all that serious. They were more like a game that I could step out of at any time, like coming out of a restless sleep in which the horror, however endless it seems, is not quite real.

There were rare moments too in which my mind seemed to contain its own looming horror. What this horror was, how I could use it, and against whom, wasn't clear to me.

My novel was a testimony to all these chimeras. It lay in front of me, tangible and beautiful. This was enough for me to consider it finished. There it was, perfect, or, putting it differently, fulfilled.

Involuntarily, I imagined the catch of breath in the ancient theatre of the Acropolis, dozens of centuries ago, when Agamemnon's wife, at the moment when she welcomes with flattering words the husband she will murder a few moments later, utters the ambiguous phrase, 'Your life is finished.'

In my mind, my novel was perfect, finished, which meant both beautiful and at the same time dead.

'Ah, so it's a trilogy,' said my editor at the publishing house, taking the manuscript. 'Is *The Three-Arched Bridge* the overall title, or . . .'

'It's the title of the first part, and also of the whole trilogy.'

He had the bad habit, when receiving a manuscript, of leafing through it in the author's presence.

'So the second part is about the dominions of the great pashas,' he went on, as if talking to himself. 'A very attractive theme, interwoven like that. And the third . . . ah, the third is about Boris Pasternak . . .' he exclaimed in astonishment. I wanted to say to him, why not? As I was on the list myself, didn't I have the right . . . or maybe for that very reason I had no right . . .

But instead I thought, how the hell did he notice the name of Pasternak in all of that 600-page manuscript? He gave the explanation himself.

He smiled, without raising his eyes from the text. 'I'm looking at the start of a section,' he muttered. 'Doctor, Doctor Zhivago . . . it was as if a sick Russia were in search of a doctor . . . Well put.'

I sighed silently in relief. I felt again the urge to offer the explanations that had died in my mouth as soon as I entered his office.

I had wanted for many years to write something about my student life in Moscow. The novel even started like that, but wandered off. It was lightweight, lyrical. A writers' holiday home on the Baltic coast, near Riga. Beautiful twilights. A ping-pong game, a girl called Birgita, like half the girls of Latvia. Nobody predicted the great split in the socialist camp, which would come with the Moscow autumn, or called for a doctor . . . Zhiv—

I sensed that I was talking too much, against my habit, but as anyone might when they feel guilty.

'In short, Pasternak is there quite by accident.' On hearing Pasternak's name, the editor nodded in satisfaction.

'Those five or six lines were really brilliant. Quite enough to describe the situation.'

I tried to imagine his surprise when he saw that it wasn't five or six lines, but almost half the novel.

I would have preferred not to continue the conversation about this damned novelist.

The book went on to describe the approach of the Moscow autumn. In other words, an ordinary story involving girls, with the Pasternak rally in the middle.

In truth, it was a girl in the second year with

tear-filled eyes who attracted my attention at the rally. Someone told me she was Pasternak's niece, so there was a reason for her eyes to be filled with tears as she heard the shouts against her uncle.

But, even without this information, this woman's tears made a deeper impression on me than seemed called for. Indeed, I liked to take Pashko Vasa's famous lines 'Weep, women, weep, young girls, with those lovely eyes that weep so well' as an invitation to describe Albanian history differently. Not in the light of medieval archives, Vatican documents or Marxist concepts, but in another way, seen through women's tears.

The problem was that for so long we had been unable to weep.

Any fool could tell I really was talking too much, but this didn't stop me.

'The girl who was crying in fact wasn't Pasternak's niece, but this didn't make any difference.'

I had the impression that the editor wasn't listening, and his mind was elsewhere.

Perhaps he too felt bad. (Doctor, I'm not well. Doctor Zhivago.)

It seemed to me we were both eager to say goodbye.

On the street, after I had left, I recalled the details of the conversation, but couldn't work out whether he had felt doubtful about the text or not. Maybe I had sown these doubts myself, with those unnecessary explanations.

These explanations still ran through my mind. That girl with the tears wasn't Pasternak's niece, but the daughter of his lover, a certain Olga Ivinskaya, a beautiful fair-haired woman that everyone was talking about in those days, one could imagine why.

The girl was nineteen, and called Irina, but these facts not only changed nothing for the better, but perhaps made things worse.

One month later, when I went to the editor's office to receive an answer, I noticed at once that familiar stiffness that authors recognise when an editor has reservations about a book.

Unlike last time, he avoided my gaze.

When I looked down at his hands, I thought I saw them shake a little.

This isn't possible, I thought. If anybody's hands should shake here they should be mine.

'This is a special book,' he said, looking side-long. And then, as if he had made a discovery, he added, 'What you might call three novellas, or novels, with a common thread.'

'Yes,' I repeated softly. 'A common thread. I even thought at one time of calling it a triptych, but . . .'

'Perhaps triptych would be going too far . . . but there is certainly a link.'

'There is,' I repeated.

He said something about the first part, *The Three-Arched Bridge*, stressing the number three which suggested what you might call the structure of the book.

'Exactly,' I replied. 'Three arches, as it were, symbolic.' How banal, what I was saying.

Then it was he who said, 'a symbolic three'.

For a while we dwelt again on the word 'triptych', and then with a certain lack of enthusiasm moved on to the second part, the novella about the severed head of Ali Pasha Tepelenë, placed in the 'traitor's niche' for the crowds to stare at. Traitor to the state, infidel, Zhivago.

I would never have believed that in pronouncing the words 'traitor's niche', instead of wanting the conversation to end as soon as possible, I would be doing all I could to prolong it.

The severed head of the rebel vizier, placed on display at the centre of the Ottoman Empire, under the curious eyes of the inhabitants of the capital. Its frozen gaze. The stare of the crowd. The terror between the two.

It was Professor Çabej who had explained to me on a journey to Istanbul the meaning of the phrase in Ottoman Turkish, *ibret tashe*, 'Learn from suffering.' It was so like what happened everywhere.

Astonishingly, I didn't skirt round this conversation. Beheaded by the KGB. Groan, doctor, doctor.

The conversation grew more dangerous as it went on. Then the question flashed into my mind. Sure, I wanted to put off talking about the third part, with the sensitive girl and the Pasternak campaign, but why did he?

He had the state to back him up and could bare his teeth at any moment.

'My dear friend, you have a few troubling bits here. I shall have to go back to this text again, twice, even twelve times if necessary.'

Still he behaved in this circumspect manner, as if this discomfort, even debacle, was not something caused by me, but by both of us together.

His right hand again began to tremble a little, and there was a kind of plea in his eyes, as if we shared a common worry. He moved on from

Pasternak, as I had done, without realising he was getting into even deeper water.

I could barely restrain myself from butting in. What's the matter with you, man? But, as so often happens when under pressure, I somehow remembered that mysterious, little-discussed region of fear felt by editors, those people we authors find frightening.

D.D. (Double Dilaver, as we called him) had distantly alluded to such a thing. 'You authors generally badmouth us, but not many understand the troubles we have.'

I hadn't paid him much heed, for this was a matter of closed meetings of the state's loyalists, which were forbidden to the rest of us. These were the guards who kept watch on us, so their gripes reminded me of the proverb about a well-horsed rider complaining at not having stirrups.

According to Double Dilaver, it wasn't like that at all. There was an exhaustive investigation in the wake of every banned book. Question:

how could you as an editor fail to understand that this author is spreading poison? The question was blunt, but simple at least, as was the reply. I was naive, blinkered, because of my shallow understanding of Marxism-Leninism. I'm guilty. Let the party punish me.

Unexpected things could happen if the matter was put the other way round, if in place of 'How did you fail to understand,' the question was 'How did you understand?'

This question would inevitably cause some puzzlement, and the matter then became complicated. The silence would deepen. So would suspicion. 'How did you come to such a perverse interpretation of the text? What were you thinking of when you asked the author to cut all traces of the sultan's jealousy, and especially his homosexual tendencies? Well? Is it our job to defend the Turkish sultan or what?'

We carefully skirted the second part of the book, to approach inevitably the danger zone:

Moscow. It was hard for us to hide our shared anxiety. His voice became strangely soft as he told me that in this book we were up against two . . . things . . . or, rather . . . strands, or tendencies, or whatever you might call them . . . with the Soviet state on one hand and the writer Boris Pasternak on the other. The particular thing here was that both sides, the state and the writer, were equally deplorable. We couldn't say one was worse than the other. 'But you as an author, and we alongside you, are with neither of them. We are, as you might say, neither . . . nor . . . In short we don't care if they go at each other hammer and tongs.'

Neither, nor, I thought, surprised at this manner of expression.

In fact, it was all more or less as I had expected, when I'd imagined how I could justify the book. I was simply a spectator. I was present after everything had been decided and I had no business to interfere.

Impartiality was usually inadvisable, and, in that my name had been mentioned in this deadly whisper, my own impartiality might not seem very convincing.

Neither, nor, I thought again, more calmly. He looked me straight in the eye before continuing with his explanation.

'Of course, there was no way we could take the side of the Soviet state, whatever happened. We know all about them. But we can't support this writer either.'

I couldn't grasp whether he was driving at something or merely wanted to suggest to me that I had unconsciously (of course unconsciously) taken the side of the writer.

'Not the side of the Soviet state, of course not,' he continued, shaking his head, as if to say 'dear, oh dear'. 'Especially since there have been rumours of certain nostalgic types, who say things like how I miss those Russian songs, and so on. Like the rumours that spread just before a conspiracy is discovered. Perhaps you heard about the arrest just recently in the publishing house.'

We continued to stare fixedly at one another. So this was what he was worried about. Now it wouldn't be a surprise to hear him say, what made you choose this subject, at this moment? Or worse, how did you get me mixed up in this?

But instead he went on speaking against Pasternak.

'Let the Soviet state go to hell, but, please, we can't hold with Pasternak either. No way,' he repeated, still staring at me.

'Of course not,' I replied. 'I don't think there's any such suggestion in my book.'

'I didn't mean that,' he interrupted me. 'Of course nobody would think of such a thing. Never in a hundred years.'

I suggested that the very confrontation between the two inevitably created a kind of empathy or pity for the isolated individual.

'Precisely,' he burst out. 'Pasternak is on his

own. Insulted by one-sixth of the planet, as you have described in this book. Even more, by half of it. And he keeps silent.'

Exactly . . . You, that is Pasternak, keep silent. And this seems something terrible and hopeless. The eyes of the crowd are upon you, some with hatred, others with contempt, and a few with sympathy . . . It doesn't occur to anyone amid all this misery that you, or anybody to whom such a thing happens, might in fact be experiencing something very rare, an unprecedented mingling of grief and wisdom, the intoxication of your own downfall.

You snort to yourself that these are a savage, mindless people, and at that moment, to your own surprise, as if you have grasped the lineaments of an impenetrable mystery, you are gripped by a perverse respect for them.

You have seen them shouting, laughing their heads off at celebratory rallies, and suddenly they turn on you, sinister and threatening, and you shout back, 'Insult me, turn your rage on me, maybe one day you'll thank me for giving you this chance.'

Despite our efforts to linger on the easy part of the novel: the Baltic coast, dusk, the ping-pong game, the pensive gaze of the girl as she followed the bouncing ball . . . nothing could prevent the approach of the grim Moscow autumn.

I could almost feel the pages turn in the silence. We came to the part with the groan. *Doctor . . . doctor . . . of Russia.* The editor didn't express the same enthusiasm as before. Hang on, I thought, looking at the expressionless face I took to be a protective mask, at least he hasn't said anything bad. That was some consolation.

Then came the wild nights with drunken writers revealing the subjects of their books, and a Mongolian who threw himself from the fourth floor.

'What do you think about that girl with her eyes full of tears?' I asked him.

'Which girl?'

'The one I thought was Pasternak's niece, who was in fact his lover's daughter.'

He nodded. It was the third time I had recalled this passage, even reminding him of her name, Irina, but I didn't mind appearing scatterbrained. That description seemed to me to offer salvation and I had no intention of letting go of it so easily. This section was again about girls' tears and their fluttering eyes; the atmosphere recalled the start of the novel. It was in short a novel about memory.

'That was her real name, Irina, and as if it wasn't enough for her mother to be mixed up with Pasternak, she was engaged to a Frenchman.'

'Uh-huh,' he went, a bit surprised. Apparently he hadn't remembered this detail from the novel, so I explained that I hadn't enlarged on this theme, not to weigh down the book.

'Uh-huh,' he went again, with a casualness I found rude.

'That's what we called him, the French fiancé,

frantsuskii zhenikh,' I stubbornly continued. 'At that time engagements to foreigners weren't taboo. You could arrive at customs at Tirana airport and declare the tape-recorder or television you'd brought from Moscow, and just as naturally point to the foreign girl by your side, and this here is my fiancée.'

'I heard something of that sort,' he said.

'It seems incredible now, but that's what it was like then, even with the woman holding a chubby little baby in her arms. Interesting, isn't it?'

He responded with a look that really was, well, interesting, and I hurried to add a firm 'but . . .'

'But in fact this was only true for us, boys of the East as you might call us, whereas for Westerners things were different. So Irina's "French fiancé" was a real curiosity.'

'Obviously,' he said with clear impatience. He was recovering his assumed bravado.

Irina, despite those tear-filled eyes, had still not grasped the true importance of the scandal in those first days. Indeed, as we heard from Dalia Epshteyks, one of her friends who liked to tease the Balts on our course, it was Irina herself who had told the grotesque story of a woman on the trolleybus who, annoyed with the conductor, had shouted, 'What do you take me for? I'm not dirt, understand, I'm not some *zhivaga*.'

'Well, well,' said the editor, still leafing through the pages of the text in whose margins he had scribbled his notes.

In the text, the worldwide vilification of Pasternak continued.

'Hmm,' he went, after his next silence, and added, 'but this Pasternak, he was no angel himself.'

I recalled again the famous telephone call from Stalin. Of all the faults ascribed to Pasternak, his response to this phone call, especially the phrase, 'We are different, Comrade Stalin,' left the bitterest aftertaste.

I was waiting for him to mention this very

thing, but remembered that Mandelstam and Anna Akhmatova were, like Ernest Koliqi, among the most strictly forbidden names in Albania, as this editor surely knew.

'Pasternak was no angel,' he went on, and I was expecting him to say that it wouldn't be a bad thing to emphasise this, whereupon I would ask in reply, how far should this emphasis go, because never in history had a man ever been so insulted. And he might have answered that this was true, but I had rather made light of these insults, so that . . . but there was no telling where this would lead.

Fortunately, he did not plunge into this morass. He moved his lips, as if to say tut-tut, what can we do, but said no more.

There had been no end to the tide of insults, which swept away anything in its path. Each person had every right to look to their own skin.

Suddenly the question of whether or not he knew that I was on this accursed list flashed

42

through my mind, alongside the idea that the crux of the matter, before it had anything to do with literary spies or references to Dante's *Inferno*, concerned myself: was I comparing myself to Pasternak or not?

'We are different, Comrade Stalin.'

A kind of apathy, the sign of extraordinary weariness, swept over me. This too will pass, I thought, as he continued to leaf through the text. I couldn't clearly see which parts he'd finished with, and which were still to come.

Finally the torture came to an end. He closed the file with a few words along the lines of: 'That's enough for now. Let's wait and see what the others say.'

It could be imagined who the others were, but none of them could be identified precisely. The office of the Central Committee, and maybe other offices that nobody knew about. The editor's boss, and of course his boss's boss, above whom there might be yet another boss.

I left the office with a kind of numb relief. I thought it was perhaps better if I didn't know all the details. After all, the torment was over, and any respite was welcome.

Unlike on other occasions, I wouldn't have to wait long for a final decision on publication. Indeed, I secretly hoped the wait would be longer.

I thought of my manuscript only occasionally, and not with impatience. The prosecutors are working on it, I thought. The word 'prosecutor' strangely summed up all the people who might be dealing with the novel.

When the editor phoned me, I thought, already?

As if he knew what I was thinking, he added that there had been a bit of space at the printers in the last few weeks, and my book had been lucky.

'Ah, so it's been published?' I asked in surprise.

'It's been published, of course,' he replied,

clearly pleased. I could call round for the first copy about midday.

I restrained myself from saying, half in jest, that the prosecutors had been fast this time.

But I kept this until we met.

He looked at me in some astonishment.

'What prosecutors?' he said. 'The prosecutors will look at it now that it's published.'

So the matter was still not closed.

'The prosecutors don't often intervene,' he said. 'Only if the law is broken. To tell the truth, it's not clear to me either . . . but forget about that. Congratulations on the book.'

I picked it up in some puzzlement. This was a familiar feeling, quite different from what everybody imagines, not at all pleasant, but the contrary. There was something cold and threatening about the book, as if it wasn't my own. As if its appearance in public print had taken it from me.

Out of an instinct of self-defence, I wanted to stop the publication.

As happens in moments of panic, my mind ran to impossible things, turning the book back into a manuscript and then unwriting it.

After this surreal scene, I soon imagined myself telling the Pasternak story in oral form, like some bard of the mountains.

In Stockholm spoke the evil envoy.

However naive and childish this picture, I went on first in the style of the bards of the north, and then of the singers of my home town.

Rise Maksim Gorky from your grave
Or Moscow will be the tsar's slave.

Pull yourself together, I thought. Instead of such nonsense better deal with the essential . . . the crux. They tell you this and that, but let's look for the crux. This . . . the crux . . . was out in public now and there was no pulling it back.

When Zinaida learned his fate
She held her hands and wept in grief.

But instead of calling a halt, I replaced the name of Pasternak's wife with Irina, the weeping girl . . . and then even with my wife Helena . . .

The editor watched me leaf through the book as if I were looking for something. Now that I was seeing it with a different eye, the first part of the book, that blessed beginning with ping-pong on the shore of the Baltic, seemed very short. But the part with Dante's *Inferno* in contrast seemed endless. I might have avoided that damned comparison of the floors of the Institute with Dante's circles, I thought. Especially the mention of the writer spies . . . I looked at the book in astonishment, as if I hadn't written it myself. All right if it's just me, but that idiot editor might have noticed it, not to mention the prosecutors.

I put down the book and asked what was happening with the arrests at the publishing house.

'Nasty business,' he replied. 'The investigations just go deeper and deeper.'

'The prosecutors must have a lot of work,' I said with pretended casualness.

'Well . . .' he said, implying that after the exposure of the conspiracies in the army and industry, others were to be expected. 'So nobody can feel safe.'

So that's where we are, I thought. Everybody knew that each of us had to look after our own selves, but I hadn't expected this to come from the character in front of me. Astonishingly, he didn't avoid this sensitive subject. 'Conspiracies turn up where you would never imagine them,' he went on. 'After the oil industry, for instance, might come the chrome mines.'

'Yes, but what about the kind encouraged from abroad, by the Soviets, for example?'

'They will be seen for what they are,' he said, implying that he knew something but couldn't say any more.

Well, I thought. This is perhaps why the prosecutors themselves didn't know which way they were facing.

He lowered his voice. 'Considered from this angle, your novel is coming out at just the right moment. Nobody has ever given Moscow such a drubbing in literature.'

'Really?' I said.

He spoke even more softly. 'The Soviet-lovers have been somehow forgotten recently. Ours, the ones we have here, did what they could. They were always in the Soviet Union in their own minds. They longed for Moscow, the Russian winter, and all those other things that you know better than I do. But this novel puts a stop to all that. We see a different sort of Moscow here.'

'Of course it's different,' I said, 'totally.' But I might have left out the writer spies, I thought. Not for any specific reason, but they were so like our own. In fact, if we start looking for similarities, there are a lot of them, not to say that

49

everything is the same. That's understandable, we were part of the same family for so long. With the same customs, quirks, call them what you like. This thought seemed to calm me. If it was a matter of resemblance or imitation, you might say that the two sides gave and took equally, or Moscow probably took the very worst from Tirana.

My thoughts moved faster and I turned the pages more quickly. I was heedlessly skimming over other dangerous portions of the book, besides the spies.

They can resemble each other as much as they like, I thought. The most important thing is that I mustn't be like them. Not like Pasternak or anyone else.

And so, I wasn't . . . Damned if they could say I was like him. Not him or anybody.

I am different, Comrade Stalin. From Akhmatova, from Nadezhda Mandelstam, I mean, her husband, and especially from Pasternak. And as

for that Swedish list of nominations, let them
wave it about as much as they like. Anybody can
make any sort of list.

Something interrupted my frenzy. Was it a
word or ironic smile from the editor as he watched
me furiously turning the pages? No, it was something worse than that. The irony came from the
book itself, a phrase in it, which lay in ambush
about halfway through the fourth chapter. I
wanted to pretend I hadn't seen it and move on,
but I couldn't. It was the letter of a Russian girl,
which I had included as if the devil were at my
elbow. In fact, it was a PS at the foot of the letter.
'They were talking on the radio all day yesterday
about a writer who had turned traitor and it
reminded me of you.'

I froze. With my own hand I had inserted
this horror. I had tried harder to avoid this kind
of thing more than anything else. It meant I
had equated myself with Pasternak, in other
words the writer who had turned traitor, and it

was now 1976, the second year in which I was on the same list as he had been. This had been made public not by some bourgeois provocateur, but my beloved girl in Moscow, one of those whose caresses and sweet words were unforgettable. 'My little traitor, let the Russian people insult you and all the Albanians, but you have me.'

Oh no, I thought, I called myself an idiot again and mentally begged the girl to stop, calling her *moy blyad*, a prostitute, and for the first time in my life I was ready to use this word against art itself.

I had no need to read further to see the book's obvious treason. All that grimness of Moscow with its spies and circles of hell, and then the cholera epidemic described in detail in the book's last pages, automatically became transplanted to Tirana.

What have you done to me? I asked myself, the girl of the letter and my own art, simultaneously.

But from the book came a challenge, a game of cat and mouse, careless but determined. Catch me if you can! It's up to you.

For a short time I stared into space, as if caught in a trap. At that moment, it really was within my power to prevent that fateful step. I could tell the editor that I would look at it one more time and make improvements. Even at my own expense.

I could halt the publication, but ah, it was beyond my strength.

It took only an instant to realise that I couldn't do it.

Never, I thought. Never in the world.

I thought of the final pages of the epilogue, in which, as if the desolation of the epidemic were not enough, I myself, now deceased, rode through Moscow on horseback, together with the girl who wrote the letter. It was for her that I had risen from the grave, because I had given her a promise, as in the old ballad of Doruntina, which I had wanted to rewrite for years but could not.

I felt the weariness of death envelop me again. I recalled the epilogue to the book, but instead of giving me more reason to pause, it made me think that if it was a matter of finishing, in other words dying, it would be good fortune to die for this miracle.

The intoxication of my own downfall returned to me more strongly than ever, and with it there came back the ambiguous words about the man who was finished, that is perfected and at the same time dead, as a woman had said of her husband, just before killing him, 2,500 years ago in the theatre of the Acropolis.

This epilogue contained both these things, perfection and death. This destiny again and again governs art too, which cannot be perfected without being finished.

PART
TWO

PASTERNAK DOT com. And so on. Osip Mandelstam, Irina Emelyanova, Yosif Stalin dot com. Anna Akhmatova. Nikolai Bukharin. Nadezdha Mandelstam. Olga Ivinskaya. Georges Nivat. Zinaida Nikolayevna. Anne Nivat. Café Saint-Claud (since vanished). Peredelkino dot com.

Incredible.

The word was easy to say, but impossible to grasp in all its dimensions. What was incredible was the passage of time. It was 2015, at one o'clock, in a small restaurant in the rue Monsieur-le-Prince in Paris. Helena and Irina Emelyanova were waiting for me so that we could have lunch together.

(Do you see that girl with the sad eyes? etc. etc.) It was none other than her, whom I had mentioned in my novel long ago.

It had already been incredible, *nyeverovatno*,

when Irina from my Moscow years had turned up at our apartment in Paris, at 63, boulevard St Michel.

The words 'I couldn't believe my eyes' had been said in French, Russian and Albanian and I wasn't surprised to see her lift her hand to these eyes to wipe away at last those lovely tears from the last century.

'Irina, can you imagine what I'm writing?' I hoped that Helena would have told her already that I was writing about Pasternak again, but this time only three minutes of his life.

If Helena hadn't said this to her already, in order to avoid the slightest foretaste of disappointment (such a brief revisit to Pasternak?), I would have to explain that these three minutes were the famous telephone call with Stalin. If she was still not satisfied (why just those three minutes?), I would explain my reasoning.

After wearing myself out trying to calculate how many minutes there can have been in

Pasternak's seventy years of life (sometimes I reckoned thirty million, sometimes forty), I thought of how I could justify this obsession of mine: my respect, if only indirect, for one of the interlocutors, Pasternak or, God preserve us, Stalin? Or was it the mystery surrounding one or other of them or maybe both, not to mention myself? Or none of us?

I thought I could work it out. Sometimes I was nearly there, but then the answer would elude me.

Those three minutes! They had happened, they had been . . . (What word can you use for three minutes in the distant year of 1934?) So, they had happened on a June afternoon, thirty years before I heard about them when I was twenty-one years old, in my first month in Moscow. These three minutes were often mentioned when the storm raged round Pasternak. They'd been forgotten for so long, and some people asked why they were now being remembered.

Others said that they were being recalled now because they were vital to delivering the final blow against the poet.

The endless speculation about them returned again and again to that unforgettable afternoon. There were many different accounts. I myself had identified thirteen versions. Why did these three minutes so obsess me?

I couldn't say why, but still my mind returned to them again and again.

The conversation was beyond improbable, beyond impossible, an evil omen come from another world. The poet and the tyrant should never have been put together. But an authoritative voice ensured that it happened. Whether they wished it or not, they were together, two manifestations of the same thing: power. Slaves of each other in the same circle of Dante. Torturing each other, each the other's downfall, whether for three minutes or for as many centuries or millennia was of no importance.

The telephone call had to do with a mystery that we all share in. The poet entered the stage not of his own free will but because the laws of tragedy demanded it.

So, there were three: Pasternak, Stalin and Mandelstam. Two poets and the tyrant between them. The first thought was an exciting prospect: the two poets could unite to bring down the tyrant.

Both secretly despised this tyrant. Mandelstam had called him 'the Kremlin mountaineer'. Pasternak was said to have described him as a dwarf with the body of a fourteen-year-old and the face of an old man. Now they had him in their grip, two against one, and could destroy him with all the cruelty that poets know how to use.

But the tyrant also had his tricks. Stalin knew how to divide the powerful pair of poets. The myth about Pasternak abandoning his friend was calculated to echo down the generations. A quarter of a century later, in that Moscow autumn of the Nobel Prize, it bore its first fruit. Half a century later, in the third millennium, it was still in circulation everywhere. In Paris, Tokyo, New York. The conversation was analysed in detail, second by second. The words, the pauses between them, the breathing. The telephone ringing, the first word uttered. The reply. The first silence. Doubt. The continuation, which reports claim was like the beginning. Sort of. But later not. Then the similarity returned.

There was good reason why the puzzle started with one question – whether the tyrant defeated the poet – and ended with another one – whether or not the tyrant was defeated by the people.

A warning to be careful, take it slowly, was naturally part of this story. It was 23 June 1934 and Osip Mandelstam had just been arrested. All Moscow was talking about this. Then the telephone rang, and it was Stalin. The conversation was between him and Pasternak, but in fact there were three of them: the brace of poets, Mandelstam and Pasternak, and the tyrant facing them. Everybody's first thought was that the tyrant had both in the palm of his hand. But who was in the hand of whom?

Anyway, they were a pair. Two poets, one greater than the other. But only one tyrant.

Pairs or trios formed by poets themselves but more often by their readers are familiar.

The pairing of Mandelstam and Pasternak was genuine, almost fashionable. Everybody talked about them together, so Anna Akhmatova's question, Mandelstam or Pasternak, coffee or tea, became proverbial. Which of these two shall we talk about, dear guest? What shall we order? Coffee or tea?

There were further comparisons, some of them surprising and beyond comprehension such as the resemblance to Rosencrantz and Guildenstern, Hamlet's two friends, but often sadly appropriate: Pasternak in his dacha, Mandelstam in an exile's shack. The first always winning, the second always losing. And so on until death, which both separated them and joined them in perpetuity. Pasternak's death in his dacha, which they left to him, even after all the vilification heaped on him, perhaps because it disgraced him more than any insult. And the exiled Mandelstam's death in a hut.

The first died from the Nobel Prize, and shook the entire world, and the second from typhus and hunger, unknown to anyone. So they were different, and so were their deaths, while at the same time maybe similar.

In this world, poets are always similar, whether in the bright light of fame or in the darkness of grief.

Mandelstam and Pasternak were similar without knowing it, or wishing it.

They were almost the same age, and of average height. Their mothers were Jewish pianists who adored Rubinstein. Both born in winter. They became acquainted in 1922, and both married in the same year. They had travelled to the Caucasus, one to Georgia and the other to Armenia. They felt a kind of guilt towards the people. They were often depressed, and suffered from insomnia.

Their similarity was also reflected in the responses of others.

People loved them both.

Or neither.

They also imitated them.

There were people who wanted to be like one of them.

Others wanted to be like the other.

Still others wanted to be like both at the same time.

To understand better what happened to them, we must remember the atmosphere of the 1910s and 1920s. As if anticipating the coming unprecedented dry season of Krupskaya–Lenin, the literary world acquired an extraordinary sensitivity, both frightening and morbid, yet wonderful. Hitherto unheard-of currents of poetry, futurist, parasymbolist, acmeist, postmodernist, para-post-mystical, ceaselessly came and went. Clubs, salons, literary ladies popped up where least expected. Their manifestos were obscure, and led to incredible events. It was said of Aleksandr Blok, the most worldly poet of the time, that he had been the undeclared chairman of the Writers Association in 1923 and that he died in misery the same year. And also that he was a dandy who now and then, out of affectation, played Hamlet on the stage. Endless arguments about who was doing the worst damage to the Russian language, lawyers or dentists, were interrupted by rumours about the five Sinyakova sisters, who at some time fell in love with everyone, 'even the dervish Khlebnikov'. The latter, a few years before he died in 1922, had proclaimed himself president of the world and one of the founders of 'transrational' language.

There were plenty of summons to duels, especially round about 29 January, the day of Pushkin's duel and death. Suicides were always well received, especially as they were becoming rarer. Pasternak, although of a retiring nature, was as involved in the first, the duels, as in the second, the suicides, perhaps out of a sense of duty. Participation in poetry evenings was also almost compulsory, and posters casually announced that 'after the reading the poet Shengeli will be given a thrashing'. No doubt one of Pasternak's first phrases, as documented by his lover Ivinskaya, was similarly well received: 'I am scary. For me only evil is good.'

Nobody could escape the caprices of the time, and especially the contemporary echoes of the past. There were different opinions about Pushkin's acceptance of the invitation to the tsar's ball, at which the tsar had announced an end to the poet's disfavour. According to some this acceptance had been fatal for Pushkin, but others said that it was thanks to this invitation that Russian literature was enriched with further gems for the next ten years. This controversy was connected to the contemporary poets' attitudes to their communist bosses, first of all Stalin. Observers of literary life noticed incidentally that Pushkin's beautiful Natalia Nikolayevna and Pasternak's charming Zinaida Nikolayevna had the same patronymic. It was a short stretch of the imagination to jump from the imperial ball at which the tsar, grasping the newly returned poet by the shoulder, had said to his courtiers, 'This is my Pushkin,' to the hall of the First Congress of socialist realism 108 years later, at which Bukharin delivered the opening speech and Pasternak, a presidium member, chaired one of the sessions, while in the semi-darkness of a box Stalin kept an eye on 'his Pasternak'. This was two months after their telephone conversation. Stalin probably hoped that, however proud these writers might appear, they would bow their heads one after another, all of them without exception, from that obstinate roughneck Bulgakov to those fastidious ladies Akhmatova and Tsvetaeva, down to Platonov who seemed the most hopeless case of all.

Spies supplied information about all of them, their foibles and diseases, and their secret lovers. Pasternak for example happily enjoyed the crown of the country's leading poet. Mandelstam was more mysterious. These poets suffered from varying degrees of insomnia, at least according to two of the five S. sisters, and so on.

Stalin's flatterers might be curious to know what business these idiosyncrasies were of Stalin's. Couldn't they just be left to claw out each other's eyes?

It was easy to talk, but hard to understand what was happening in that chaos of Moscow. Uncertainty spread to the point that one day, as I passed Pushkin's statue as usual, I thought that this statue was not what he would have wanted but its very opposite.

It was a brutal thought, but I was sure that this was the case. Throughout those days I spent scribbling in the boring lectures, I was attempting to translate Pushkin's 'Monument', or more precisely its first line:

Ya pamyatnik sebe vozdvig nyerukotvorniy

I had always thought this was untranslatable, as did most of my classmates who were trying to put this into their own languages. They all got stuck at *nyerukotvorniy*, 'not made by hand', which was the key word in the line:

I raised a monument to myself
not made by hand.

Who could imagine a more stilted translation?

However you read it, as a religious perception, a challenge or blasphemy, this was an impossible claim. The poet announced that he had raised a particular kind of monument that could not be built by human hands. Thus a monument that eyes couldn't see. In short, this statue was the opposite of the monument he wanted.

So he might write:

I raised a monument to myself, the opposite
to what I wanted.

More accurately, this monument was raised not by the poet, but by other people, so he had the right to start his poem differently:

You raised a monument to me that
I didn't want.

Moscow statues conspicuously failed to resemble the people they represented. Sometimes the bronze seemed trying to do its best, but in some cases the failure was obvious.

I mentioned this one day to David Samoylov,

the translator and editor of my book of poetry that was shortly to be published in Moscow, but he looked at me doubtfully and said nothing.

I didn't like this look and wanted to retort that I could give doubtful and mysterious looks as well as anybody, especially because my classmate Stulpans had recently told me that David Samoylov was really called David Kaufman, and for God knows what reason had changed his surname.

As my book in Russian progressed, the more shadowy the figure of Samoylov became. Behind this abstracted appearance was a once important poet who had become a translator from minor languages. These words were Stulpans', but they acquired a certain connotation in my ears (reduced to translating Albanian).

Suppressing a flash of anger, I told Stulpans that his Latvian was also a minor language, but in his gentle manner he soothed away my irritation by admitting that this was true. Indeed his impression was that Albanian was held in higher esteem in Europe than the Baltic languages.

Later, again from Stulpans, I learned that Kaufman was acquainted with the circle of Pasternak and Anna Akhmatova, which pleased me particularly. I thought that the weight he carried in those circles would help my book, edited by him, to be taken more seriously.

The mystery surrounding Samoylov grew after the Pasternak scandal, when there was so much talk of the three-minute conversation with Stalin. Stulpans said to me one day, half joking, that I was the best person to provide accurate information about that phone call. It took me a while to work out that what he meant was information that might come from Samoylov, who had been involved in the same circle as Pasternak and Akhmatova, including Lydia Chukovskaya, Zamyatin and perhaps Mandelstam himself.

I said I didn't believe they were close enough friends to talk about such delicate matters.

'Close enough friends . . .' he said abstractedly. 'Listen, if anyone in Moscow can explain the riddle of that conversation, it's your David Kaufman.'

I laughed. It was then his turn to laugh. Then mine again. Were we failing to understand one another because he thought that I thought that Kaufman would ask Pasternak about the conversation?

'Why shouldn't you think that?' he replied.

'True,' I said, and he said the same, 'true'.

We stumbled over words. 'Let's be plain,' he said. Of course we should be. 'A phone call has taken place between two people. To ascertain the truth, one could ask both people, or one of them. In this case clearly the person to ask would be Pasternak. Otherwise, one might ask Stalin.'

He drew his face close to mine and frowned. 'Ask Stalin?' he muttered. 'Of course we could!'

I could frown deeper than him. The idea had now been floated. To find out what had been said on the phone that June evening in 1934, David Samoylov, my David Kaufman, wouldn't ask Pasternak or any of the acmeists, half the futurists, the five S. sisters or the pimps of Tverskoy Boulevard, but Stalin himself, because Stalin's daughter Svetlana Alliluyeva, otherwise known as Sveta Stalina, or affectionately in the family as Svetik, had long been Kaufman's lover.

'Half Moscow knew this, apart from you,' said Stulpans, wagging his finger at me in reproach. He told me the epigram of the drunkard Misha Svetlov, *Trudno lyubit printses, uzhasno muchitelniy protses* (hard to love a princess, a terrible harrowing process). Not to mention an unnamed person's ambiguous remark that sleeping with the little Stalinka was like making love to a marble effigy.

Unwittingly I had become privy to one of Moscow's most dangerous secrets. Whenever I met Samoylov, his icy expression deterred me from asking the fatal question.

Once, in a dream, he explained the story of himself and Sveta to me in halting Albanian.

'I meet Sveta at house of Mikoyan. Svetka not cold at all. She volcano. Don't you. You no ask details. They dangerous.'

I shook my head. Of course, the details would still be dangerous. However, I wouldn't ask about them but about simpler things, like that three-minute conversation with Pasternak.

But before he had heard me out, he repeated, 'Big danger.' And then I woke up.

PART
THREE

CURIOSITY ABOUT the precise number of versions of the Stalin–Pasternak telephone call was probably revived by Izzi Vishnevetsky, a post-communist Russian, in his book *Stalin and Pasternak*, published in Moscow in 2009.

The study was a kind of response, on the whole a measured one, to another Russian, Benedikt Sarnov, a well-known critic, former student of the Gorky Institute and author of the book *Stalin and the Writers*, published in 2008, also in Moscow.

After making a careful calculation, with his usual modesty, Vishnevetsky writes that there were in fact thirteen versions, not twelve as stated by Sarnov.

Because we studied at the same institution, I would be inclined to put more faith in the former Gorky student.

There were multiple versions, though two would be enough to create confusion. According to Vishnevetsky, Sarnov supplies the date and circumstances of the event with each version: Mandelstam's famous verses were written in 1933 and were read in a circle of friends in 1934. Mandelstam was arrested in May that year and detained in the Lubyanka, interrogated and possibly tortured. The Stalin–Pasternak phone call followed in June. The two speakers were located in Stalin's office in the Kremlin and Pasternak's apartment on Volkonskaya Street in Moscow.

FIRST VERSION

(*Pervaya Versiya*. All the texts use the word deriving from Latin, *versio*.)

Here is the text from the KGB archive:

Stalin's secretary Poskrebyshev made the call. *Seychas s vami budyet govorit Tovarish Stalin.* 'Comrade Stalin will speak with you now.'

And indeed Stalin took the phone:

'The poet Mandelstam was arrested a short while ago. What can you say about him, Comrade Pasternak?'

Boris evidently took fright and replied:

'I know him only slightly. He is an acmeist, but I belong to a different group. So I can't say anything about Mandelstam.'

'Whereas I can say you're a very poor comrade, Comrade Pasternak,' said Stalin, and put down the phone.

(According to Vishnevetsky, the text comes from a book by a certain Vitaly Shentalinsky, *Slaves of Freedom: The Archives of the KGB*, published in Moscow in 1995.)

There is no information about who witnessed the call.

The text would be easy to circulate as a rumour, for it is in the colloquial language of the time, and anyone who heard it would understand it.

The four occurrences in ten lines of the word 'comrade', one of the most familiar morphemes of socialism, helps in this. For anyone listening to the rumour, the report sounds like this: *Comrade* Stalin phones *Comrade* Pasternak to say that *Comrade* Pasternak was a poor *comrade*.

But anyone reading this text for the first time wouldn't gather much more from it.

An arrest is reported, as if it were already known, as it was, but not the reason for it. Considered calmly, this is no great omission. The reason for an arrest can be given or kept secret. Indeed, the arrest might have a reason or not.

Stalin, instead of telling Pasternak even indirectly the reason for this arrest (anti-Soviet activity, propaganda, etc.), asks Pasternak for an opinion about his fellow poet, and what has happened to him, almost in the words: we've arrested your friend, what do you say to that? Is this a good or bad thing?

Pasternak talks vaguely, which might be taken

as confusion, fear or a refusal to enter into this sort of discussion with the state.

At a distance of eighty years, the transcript gives rise to all sorts of questions.

Why did Stalin telephone and why was Pasternak confused? The arrest of a great poet might come as a shock in London or Paris, but not in Moscow in 1934. What did the poet and the tyrant expect of one another, where they hiding something and were they both afraid of what they were hiding?

The only clear statement in this concise text was Stalin's phrase, 'You're a very poor comrade, Comrade Pasternak.' It's not much in a ten-line text that would be studied endlessly for the rest of the century.

Not counting the words of the secretary, Poskrebyshev, who alerted the poet that Stalin was going to speak, there are only four phrases in this whole version of the conversation.

The first two belong to Stalin, who after

mentioning Mandelstam's arrest asks what the poet thinks of it. The third phrase and Pasternak's only words are the vague reply, 'I can't say anything about Mandelstam.' The fourth and final phrase expresses Stalin's contempt for the other speaker. 'You're a very poor comrade, Comrade Pasternak.'

If there is any mystery in this conversation, it lies in this closing remark, which raises the question of why Stalin made the phone call.

It was clearly not made purely to convey information. More plausibly, it was to ask for an opinion, although it could have been a test, taking a pulse, something rarely attempted by great heads of state themselves. In that case Stalin might have been more explicit. We've arrested Mandelstam. Was this wrong? Have we been hasty? Or have we waited too long?

Pasternak might have answered in several ways. Firstly: a great poet can't be arrested just like that. Secondly, let that be a lesson to everybody. And thirdly, I don't know what to say. (Don't get me mixed up in this business.) We are different.

Pasternak said the third.

Stalin's further reply in each of these cases would be easy to imagine. A great poet can't be arrested like that? That's what you think because you're of the same breed. In the second case: so we did well? Bravo! (*molodets!*) That's what the Party wants from artists, no mercy for the enemy. But the third: you're stuck for words?

There is no need to imagine the reply to the third, because we know what it was, and it is the most surprising, contradictory, unsettling and impossible of all: 'You are a poor comrade.' This reply would leave anybody aghast. Stalin is sorry for Mandelstam, because he's in the Lubyanka, handcuffed?

This brings back the questions of what we know, don't know or misunderstand in this story. Was there really a telephone conversation between the head of state and the great poet, or is it pure fiction?

One can exclude the last possibility. There really was an arrest, as reported by many sources, just as there is proof of an interrogation with one investigator or several, and of the use of torture. Finally, a death took place that is not only convincingly evidenced, but adds weight to the story.

Of the three people involved – Pasternak, Stalin and Mandelstam – we know that it was Osip Mandelstam who was arrested and sentenced, and ultimately died in exile. This sets aside every question but one. How was it that the one character whom everyone, even Stalin, finds the most moving, who inspired grief even in his lifetime, was the only one who perished?

This is no doubt one of the reasons, if not the principal one, why these events are remembered almost a century later. Endless articles and plays have been written about it, prompting fresh speculations, and the world's press still recalls that June afternoon in 1934 when Stalin made his phone call. All the descriptions end when the phone is put down, but the riddle persists. The questions continue, what really happened, and what hides behind Stalin, Pasternak and the dead man?

Anybody who takes the plunge in search of the truth, who thinks at first that thirteen versions are too many, may by the end of the case think that these are insufficient!

SECOND VERSION

Again according to Izzi Vishnevetsky, this second version is drawn from one of Benedikt Sarnov's books. The first obvious difference is that in this case the source of the testimony is provided. It is Galina von Meck, a writer, and Tchaikovsky's great-niece, and probably Mandelstam's lover. The testimony is drawn from her memoirs *As I Remember Them* and *Preserve What I Say.*

Here is the 22-line text:

It happened a short time after Mandelstam's exile . . .

It was before Osip Mandelstam's latest banishment that a small group of his friends came together to discuss what could be done. I of all the people present was the only outsider, neither poet nor writer.

At last there was a ring at the door; our host Yevgeny Khazin went to open it and came back with Pasternak. Boris looked upset, worried and nervous: 'Something awful has happened to me,' he said. 'Awful! And I behaved like a coward!' – and then he told us. That very day in the morning as he sat writing in his study the phone rang – he answered it. An unknown voice asked him if he was Comrade Pasternak. When Boris answered 'Yes' the voice said: 'Hold on, Comrade Stalin wants to talk to you!' 'I was terrified,' Pasternak said. Then Stalin's voice came on with its typical Caucasian accent. 'Is this Comrade Pasternak?' 'Yes, Comrade Stalin.' 'How in your opinion should we deal with the problem of Osip Mandelstam? What do you think we should do?'

. . . Instead of standing up for Mandelstam he fumbled, said something like, 'You know best, Comrade Stalin, it is up to you,' in answer to which Stalin's voice with a definite sneer in it said, 'Is that all you can say – when our comrades were in tight spots we knew better how to fight for them!' and put the receiver down.

The witness's identity, especially with that unusual surname, von Meck, and her position as a woman intimate with Pasternak, encourages the hope that there might be something new in this second version – something which, if not transforming the essence of the incident, deepens or dispels the fog surrounding it.

Arrest. Interrogation. Exile. Finally, death. It seems there is nothing else worth looking for in this grim story. Unless the conversation itself could be cast in doubt. The refrain is a familiar one: did that phone conversation really take place or not? The chronicles of the time do not raise the slightest doubt, and such a thing would be impossible to invent. If the incident were a fiction, suspicion would fall on one of the interlocutors, if not both. To make up this phone call would be both illogical and frightening. It would be illogical for Pasternak to invent a conversation that did him no honour. It would be frightening for Stalin, putting into circulation an invention that could be disbelieved. Several sources testify that not only did he not seek to prevent the spread of reports of the phone call, but he encouraged it. Pasternak himself said that he asked Poskrebyshev if he could talk about this sensitive conversation, and the latter replied that of course he could. Besides this, the reports were so widespread that all Moscow knew, which can only be explained by the acquiescence of the state.

There is also the question of whether there is anything we weren't fully aware of or were mistaken about.

This second version increases the impression of culpability. If in the first version Pasternak's guilt at abandoning his friend is clearly implied, here the entire weight of the conversation falls on this aspect. It is precisely this which was not fully known to us. To humiliate the poet, Stalin made a very damaging comparison, recalling his own Bolshevik friends, who didn't betray their comrades.

At first sight, the comparison leads to the moral question of who was the most generous and merciful. The essence of the conversation could be summed up in the great leader's desire for some advice, to encourage him to be lenient. The sovereign asked for this encouragement from the poet, but the poet unfortunately disappointed him.

Before analysing this disappointment, we must ask if Stalin really required Pasternak's intervention to mitigate his punishment of Mandelstam.

Another question might precede this one. Was Stalin really irritated by Pasternak's sidestep?

As mentioned earlier, the opposite might have been the case, and he may not have been annoyed but pleased.

But Stalin would not want to be seen in this light, that is pitiless. In this conversation, he wanted to appear the opposite, gentle, but nobody was helping him. His frank appeal was: help me to show mercy. But other people didn't want him like that. On the contrary, they wanted him to show savagery, so that they could subsequently vilify him.

Poor Comrade Stalin, poor little Stalin. His Georgian mother had an inkling of this when her son paid his last visit to her in the village she never wanted to leave. She was no doubt touched by all the honours and praise the whole world piled on to her son, but still she said that it would have been better if he had become a priest.

The poet and the prince. This comparison, or rather this rivalry, as old as the world itself, had become an agony under the communist order. The word 'prince' was avoided and replaced with 'leader' or 'guide', but the model was the same. We know that Lenin tried to avoid the word 'great' used of poets, so that it would be reserved for political leaders or the Marxist classics.

His use of the arid word *svyerhpisatel*, 'hyperwriter' or 'megawriter', showed his hatred for great writers. He tried to hide it, which also perhaps explains Stalin's uneasiness about them.

Not even the people closest to him, and maybe not even Stalin himself, knew how best to deal with these 'hypers', whether to treat them nicely or strike fear into them.

He couldn't understand that his suspicions of them involved fear, which had so strangely reversed its direction: not their fear of Stalin, but his of them. He knew that he could never admit to this fear, which only grew over time.

Were these 'hypers' frightening or not? Not only could nobody know the truth, but such a question should never so much as occur to anybody.

If the conversation strayed on to any similar topic, Lenin was careful, behind a mask of indifference, to listen carefully. There was for instance the case of Richard III of England, who had been a king like any other, until it occurred to Shakespeare, the 'hyper', to turn him into a monster in one of his plays.

If Richard is a dark and remote figure, then

what became fixed in Stalin's mind as 'the Gorky mystery' was similarly dark, if not more so.

Stalin had never managed to understand Lenin's deference to this writer. Before Bolshevism, Lenin had shown no sympathy for anybody, yet he entirely lost his nerve where Maksim Gorky was concerned. His instructions were clear: Gorky is to be forgiven everything, mistakes, foibles, bourgeois lifestyle as on the island of Capri, his insult to Soviet Russia in not coming back. It's strange that no explanation has ever been given for this generosity. Whenever it was alluded to, even remotely, Lenin's expression instantly froze.

In the last weeks of Lenin's life, when his ramblings showed signs of madness, Stalin tried to find out the secret. The patient's stare was as icy as ever, and his mutterings incomprehensible. There was something bad there, that should never be revealed, not to anybody. Not to Krupskaya, nor to Stalin himself. And for this reason

Gorky must never be touched, and nobody should ever think of muzzling him in the usual ways. It's the sort of secret that becomes more dangerous the more one pokes at it.

THIRD VERSION

'Did you hear that Borya Pasternak refused to help Mandelstam? I've heard this story twice. Have you heard it?'

'I know a bit. Borya himself told me. Stalin phoned him and asked, "What do you think of Mandelstam?" and Borya got scared, and said that he didn't know him well, although he'd heard that Mandelstam had been arrested. Stalin got very angry. "We never left our friends in the lurch," he said, and hung up.'

'Do you think that if he'd stood up for him . . . ?'

'Look. This sort of situation is full of all sorts of pitfalls, just as he was . . .'

'What was he risking?'

'Are these Pasternak's own words, or do they come from Viktor Shklovsky?'

'He told Maria Pavlovna himself. He was terrified to death.'

'He shouldn't have been. However brutal Stalin may be . . . still . . . Stalin was the sort of person . . . of course brutal, but still . . .'

(From a tape-recorded conversation between the two well-known literary personalities S. P. Bobrov and V. Duvakin, *Osip and Nadezhda Mandelstam*, Moscow, 2002.)

Apart from the increased bitterness towards Pasternak, there is nothing new in this version. S. P. Bobrov's malice towards the poet was well known. The question of whether this malice had always been present is more interesting. Did it increase over time, nourished by Pasternak's problematic reputation, especially after the Nobel affair?

The question of whether the envy of this former friend led to admiration for the tyrant, or whether this was a separate matter, would stimulate even keener curiosity.

'Stalin may be brutal . . . but still . . .'

This accursed 'but still' was usually a prelude to a tentatively prettified portrait of the dictator, and a corresponding implied denigration of the poet.

The question of the charisma of a poet or artist has always been a complicated one, because the day always comes when the thirst for praise and a measure of envy become publicly evident. The aura of fame, for good or ill, creates an all-enveloping illusion. Artists, whether they wish it or not, find themselves drawn into it. Opposite and facing them, also whether they wish it or not, are political leaders, patriarchs, national heroes. The phenomenon of charisma, for good or ill, operates in different ways on those two sides. There is something surprising here. The obverse side of glory, notoriety, brings down political idols, but has no power against artists. Indeed, instead of damaging them, it often makes them more attractive.

Is this a delusion? He is dissipated, chases women and likes a drink. That's his business. But does he write well? That's the main thing.

This paradox, repeated every century and under every kind of social order, posed a particular difficulty for communism.

At the start of Soviet Russia, it seemed that this grubby aura of writers and artists would evaporate of its own accord. It would be enough to reveal these people's disturbing secrets and they would pale immediately under the brilliant light of the cult of Lenin and Marx.

The wait was long, and the disappointment must have been bitter, especially after Sigmund Freud's intervention against Dostoyevsky. His famous introduction to the French publication of *The Brothers Karamazov* in Paris in 1928, which

Stalin had greatly hoped would damage the Russian decadents, besides accusing the great writer of possible parricide, had the opposite effect.

There is no information about whether Freud's study even indirectly prompted a new, surprising interpretation of the aura of artists – that is the creation of positive fame on the basis of their faults – but a writer's importance is hardly diminished if he appears to be a difficult character, cynical, dark and despairing. On the contrary he has everything to lose from being cheerful, confident, pure in heart and, above all, close to the people.

This last matter, being 'close to the people', had an especially strange effect. Mikhail Sholokhov, one of the most outstanding talents of the time, fell into this trap. His novel *Quiet Flows the Don* was declared to be a classic work of literature, even though its protagonist wasn't a positive character, as required by doctrine, but a man wavering between revolution and counter-revolution, even inclined in his heart towards the latter.

The writer himself accepted, or was forced to accept, the semi-official, semi-populist interpretation of his work as a reflection of the times, but this interpretation would hardly have taken root without some assistance from his work's obvious characteristics. Sholokhov, quite apart from the sort of person he was and the life he led, was exhibited everywhere as the model 'Soviet writer', free of any negative traits, never troubled by loneliness or a weakness for drink or women. Always cheerful and smiling, he would be photographed among his peasants of the Don, often in a collective farmer's blouse.

After World War Two, the distinguished writers of all the countries of the socialist camp underwent the painful transition from the bourgeois to the communist era. Terror and imprisonments were only the most obvious part of the picture. The inner dramas of disintegration and compromise were less visible and remain unanalysed to this day.

The communists were scared of art. The instructions of their most senior figures, including Lenin and Marx, were superficial: thousands of cultural workers racked their brains day and night to work out what Lenin meant in his only pamphlet about literature, *Party Organisation and Party Literature.*

Incredibly, nobody dared to say that this incomprehension stemmed from the fact that in this ordinary, boring book the author himself probably did not know what kind of literature he was talking about, whether party pamphlets and tracts, or literature as we know it. And a cursory glance at Karl Marx shows that a man who had dedicated his life to the violent overthrow of the world order never devotes half a page in any of his dozens of books to the trauma and remorse caused by the shedding of human blood.

Not to understand this means not only failing to learn anything from Homer and Dante, but something much worse. Karl Marx proposed for humanity a huge slaughter without adding a simple human warning: beware of qualms of conscience!

To stop at this point is to describe only half the evil. The other half that came later was even more macabre. Beware of qualms of conscience! Mercy was disdained as 'weakening of the class struggle' and described in thousands of studies, speeches and slogans of the day as a terrible death knell for the world proletariat. All the countries of the camp, from arch-Stalinist little Albania to vast China, had their distinct approach to this monstrous class struggle. In Albania, the relations between the communist regime and the two most distinguished writers who were not imprisoned, Fan Noli and Lasgush Poradeci, have still not been explained fully. Both began writing under the monarchy, and were equally famous but in different ways. The first, Fan Noli, the Shakespeare scholar, one-time conspirator and a former prime minister of Albania, ended up a bishop, but resident in the United States. As has often been pointed out, he was the only poet in Europe to have a long quarrel with his country's king. He succeeded in overthrowing Zog, King of Albania, and sentencing him to death in absentia, only to be overthrown by Zog in turn and likewise sentenced to death in absentia.

And yet, despite their Albanian–Balkanesque determination to do each other down, Noli and Zog were finally reconciled in 1960, when Albania was lost to them both.

The other poet, Lasgush Poradeci, was different in every way. His aura was erotic and mystical. Love, women, everything inhabited a largely non-existent world.

He even characterised himself as a 'bird of the skies', and there were plenty of malicious tongues to say that by using the name of King Zog, which in Albanian means 'bird', he was openly challenging the king: you are a bird on the earth, but I am a bird of the skies!

However, the Albanian king, unusually, did not envy poets. Perhaps for this reason, or perhaps because he was terrified by what he had already experienced at the hands of that other poet, Noli, he kept his distance, and the poet and the prince pretended not to notice each other.

And so, after the upheavals of the times, Lasgush Poradeci found himself in the communist era, amid all that cheering interrupted at intervals by the gunshots of firing squads. Being ill-adapted to any of this, even the firing squads, he was so removed from his times that any punishment he might receive seemed ineffective. However, so as not to leave him empty-handed, for the moment, and in expectation of more serious charges, they spread the word that he was a maniac and totally crazy.

Hoxha, the communist ruler, inexperienced in regal envy, imitated the former king in his attitude towards the two great artists. He was halfway reconciled with Noli, and continued the king's indifference towards Poradeci.

This inattention was mutual, and highly convenient for the poet, although not without its dangers. What really protected Lasgush Poradeci was his Hamlet-like mask. Even today, when the secret files are about to be opened, there is no evidence that he pretended to be mad. It is more likely that his madness was real.

His manner of speaking seemed not to belong to this world. Even more astonishingly, other people were known to alter their speech when they talked to him. First they would use the word 'sir', an otherwise extinct form of address. This was perhaps the indirect origin of the belief that perhaps he was no longer alive. This myth spread everywhere with inexplicable speed. Whenever he was mentioned, somebody would pipe up to ask whether he was alive or not. Then someone would reply that we all know about that. After this, few could be sure if what we knew was that he was alive or that he was dead.

Such gossip, and the question of whether we are more aware of poets when they are present among us or not, never appeared in print. Nor did the irritation felt by readers towards writers from Hungary and the Baltic countries, and far-away Mongolia. Were their books so bad because they were incompetent or because they were cramped by socialist realism? Why couldn't these writers cause a few scandals like in the past, involving if not murder, then at least some sensational divorce?

What was wrong? How did it start, and how would it end? Would it have an end?

Everybody sensed that a calamity had befallen literature. We have been searching for the reasons for this catastrophe, and failing to find them, down to the present day, as I write these lines, and the secret archives are at last being opened.

According to the Russian-American poet Joseph Brodsky, of the two ways of demolishing literature, the first, the frontal attack, was rejected in favour of a more devious method, the destruction of the building materials, that is the bricks (in this case meaning the writers), which would inevitably lead to the collapse of the structure.

Daily life itself, people and their language were spoiled and abused. Every nation in the great communist family had its own experience, in every aspect of life. The closure of locales considered characteristic of the old order, such as casinos, night clubs, brothels and the like, was accompanied by a reduction in the number of maniacs, lunatics, crackpots and nutcases, etc. Language had a role to play in all this, the written language of course, but especially the spoken form.

Some of the most problematic words created

unimaginable difficulties, such as 'gentleman', 'lady' or 'miss', to cite only three.

These words were rightly considered significant obstacles in the transition to communism. Each communist country had had its own experience of its language, often strange, as in the case of Albania. This little country, generally famous for its failings and backwardness, took an unexpected approach to these three words. Whereas the word 'gentleman' disappeared from currency in the very first phase of socialism, like in the Soviet Union, the word 'lady' had a certain staying power. But the nicest surprise turned out to be the word 'miss'. There was a determined effort to replace it, because in Albanian it carried the affectionate connotations of the word 'mother', especially in primary schools. Despite the annoyance it caused, it was used by tens of thousands of little children instead of the word 'teacher'.

Efforts to supplant it failed one after another.

The children stubbornly continued to call their teachers 'miss'. It was this army of countless toddlers that proved indomitable, and the word 'miss' with its striking elegance became permanently enshrined in the Albanian language.

Unfortunately and irresponsibly, no attention has been paid by students of Albanian language and literature to this triumph, as touching as it was prophetic.

In a broader sense, all human life was faced with bleak challenges. Besides the disappearance of late-night bars, as mentioned above, the grotesque characters that literature increasingly resorts to when under threat became increasingly rare. As did beautiful women, whose grace might cautiously inspire some love story. In the tedious rooms of the Writers' Union, people looked in vain for writers who might make some impression.

Among those who were by chance spared prison, writers emerging from the working class or from orphanages listened in stupefaction to the accounts of Soviet literature from their few colleagues who had been invited to Moscow for celebrations.

In little Albania, maddened by Stalinism, Lasgush Poradeci achieved that luxurious state of being poised between life and death. What might poets in Budapest and Moscow expect? The shy deer of art were scattered and hunted down mercilessly, and could not easily find each other.

Nevertheless, during this period of somnolence, history records all kinds of curious things: surprising characters in the middle of Moscow, railway stations, huts and places of exile with unheard-of names such as Vtoroya Reka ('second stream'). And interrogators, not one, but two or more. Then something never seen in print, but only heard, a frightening thing in the case of Mandelstam. Eleven people heard it, and Mandelstam, bound in handcuffs, had to supply their names.

At this time all sorts of extraordinary verses in idiosyncratic forms of Russian were circulating everywhere.

Two famous lines from Fyodor Sologub:

> *V polye nye vidno nyi zgi*
> *Slushitsa krik pomogi!*
> The field lies desolate and black.
> A cry for help is heard!

Another line, this time from Mandelstam:

> *No lyublyu etu kurvu Moskvu.*
> But I love this whore Moscow.

Another, anonymous:

> Life is over, but I don't know about death.

After the first rumours about the three-minute Stalin–Pasternak telephone call, few people would have imagined that the catalyst for this conversation might have been a poem. It was more likely to have been after-dinner chatter. Even when they realised that the expression 'Kremlin mountaineer' was at the root of the problem, before they thought of the poem people wondered if the word 'mountaineer' referred to him climbing to the summit of the Kremlin or to the fact that he was from Georgia.

Whichever it was, the Kremlin mountaineer or the Georgian mountaineer, either would have given Stalin sleepless nights because these were words that should never have been thought or said. It was like the mystery of Gorky, when a few phrases of the famous writer, spoken and written many years previously, had to be erased without trace, and even their erasure forgotten.

This incident happened at the beginning of the century, when Maksim Gorky, already famous, had written that during a trip to London he had happened to be present at a meeting at which the future leader of the Russian Bolsheviks, 'a certain Ulyanov, preening like a cockerel and with a screeching voice', had spoken about revolution.

It is unlikely that Stalin ever learned about these poisonous words from Lenin himself before he died in 1924. But he no doubt learned of them immediately after Lenin's death, and also of the way in which they had been consigned to oblivion. This was done in an unusual, indeed unprecedented, manner, nothing like the silence enforced by a bullet. On the contrary, the great writer was indulged with a whole array of tokens of attention, compliments and sentimental gifts.

It would have taken Stalin a long time to understand this kind of favouritism. The tenderness of the harsh leader towards the writer probably also had an emollient effect, and as the years passed Gorky's venomous remarks will have become impossible to believe.

Ten years later, in 1934, Stalin would be faced with a similar fear. His phone call to Pasternak could be nothing but a cry of panic, and so would have many secrets behind it.

Not for nothing, three-quarters of a century later, are there still questions about what had happened. Were there arrests, interrogations, with one investigator or many?

Some of these questions may seem simple, like the one about Osip Mandelstam's investigators. One investigator or many, it was of no importance. Nevertheless, people would be amazed to learn that there were in fact two investigators, and that one of them, Arkadiy Furmanov, was totally different from the other, Nikolai Shivanov, as if he had arrived from another planet. A bogus investigator? From another era? A figure from the unconscious, dressed in the suit of an investigator?

It was more than that. Arkadiy Furmanov

was a loyal friend of the poet and at the same time the person who adopted the role of the investigator in the sessions when Mandelstam, anticipating his arrest, had rehearsed answers to questions, so as not to fall into traps. It was the first time that anything like this had happened in Russia.

There were many things that happened for the first time, and many others that happened for the last time. These latter were even more terrifying, such as the telephone call that never took place, after the end of the conversation with Stalin. Pasternak had grabbed the receiver in search of a final explanation, but there was nobody at the other end of the line, until Poskrebyshev's chill voice informed him that he was never to dial that number again, because it no longer existed. 'Do you understand me?' he had said. 'This number was created for a single conversation, which has now taken place.'

FOURTH VERSION

Viktor Shklovsky, another distinguished man of letters, expressed to B. Duvakin the same opinion as that of S.P. Bobrov (the third version).

'He [Pasternak] had correspondence with Stalin, talked to him on the phone, and didn't defend Mandelstam. Do you know this story?'

'No – he didn't defend him?'

'Exactly. Stalin phoned Pasternak and asked, what do they say about Mandelstam's arrest? Pasternak himself told me that he got confused and replied:

' "Yosif Visarionovich, since you have phoned me, let's talk about history and poetry."

' "I am asking you what they're saying about Mandelstam's arrest."

'He said something else. Then Stalin said,

"If they arrested a friend of mine, I would bend over backwards to help him."

'Pasternak replied:

' "Yosif Visarionovich, if that is what you're phoning about, I have already bent over backwards."

'To this, Stalin replied:

' "I thought you were a great poet, but you're just a big fraud."

'And he put down the phone. Pasternak himself told me this, and wept.'

'So he simply got flustered . . .'

'Of course he got flustered. He might have said to Stalin, let me deal with this person. If he had wanted to. And Stalin might have let him go. But he got confused. So, you see, that is what happened.'

(B. Sarnov doesn't comment on the curious assertion that Pasternak had correspondence and further telephone conversations with Stalin.)

The final note is from Izzi Vishnevetsky. He rightly criticises Benedikt Sarnov for not explaining the origin of the 'new, interesting fact' that there had been correspondence and other telephone calls between Stalin and Pasternak. In the sixth paragraph, which starts with the words, 'He said something else,' it isn't clear which of the two, Pasternak or Stalin, said that 'something else'.

There are two gaps in the text of the fourth version.

Pasternak himself is the source of this muddle.

I have explained the Gorky mystery, and also the secret of the two investigators. However, neither the mystery nor the secret help the poet. It seems that Pasternak is failing. The interpretation of the telephone call runs more to his discredit than in his favour.

For some time there was hope that the source of Mandelstam's denunciation would be revealed.

The presence of an informer always adds weight and drama to the story of a victim. According to the American novelist Robert Littell, there was an initial denunciation made by a woman, the stage actor Zinaida Zaytseva Antonovna, probably the poet's lover. But there is something else that robbed the denunciation of its weight: the actor was extremely naive, and even unaware of what she'd done. In Chapter Ten of his book *Stalin's Epigram*, Littell relates an almost incredible scene in which the actor blithely tells her colleagues about the incident on 20 May 1934, when in the evening after the theatre rehearsals an agent of the Cheka had knocked on the door of her dressing room to express gratitude for her loyalty to Stalin. The actor was surprised and the Chekist asked her what reward she would like, a passport to travel abroad, a trip to Rome or Paris, or leading roles in the theatre. The actor replied that she had only done her job and wasn't asking for favours, but the Chekist said that a refusal might be misconstrued. So the actor asked for help in the divorce case against her husband, and to his remark that the organs of security knew how to express gratitude for those who 'work for us', she replied, 'I didn't know I was working for you.'

This reduction of the drama of the denunciation, from whatever angle it was viewed, harmed Pasternak, if only indirectly.

But there is something not quite right about this story. Nobody casts doubt on the actual telephone call, but the question arises of whether it had any part to play, for good or ill. In other words, how would the poet appear before the eyes of the prince, history and his own conscience?

The paradox of the ambivalence of the investigators goes further, and spreads over the entire case. The ambivalence starts with the arrests. Mandelstam's arrest in 1934 wasn't the first or the only one, as most people might think. Indeed, there were not just two arrests, as there were two investigators, but three or four. During the Civil War, Mandelstam was arrested twice as a Bolshevik suspect, once by officers of General Wrangel's White Army, and once by Georgian Mensheviks.

He was exiled as many times as he was arrested. Only his death happened once.

That his arrest in 1934 wasn't his first is easy to understand in a country like Soviet Russia.

His final arrest was in 1938, followed by that lonely lady, death.

Such a long time had passed since June 1934. What had happened meanwhile? Where had all these people been in these four years? Where had Mandelstam himself been?

That the calendar had gone awry was the least of it. Human minds, with their tendency to compress events, had merged the years 1934 and 1938. In such cases, the truth can only be discovered by returning to the basic facts, the times and places when events took place. As for the time, Mandelstam's arrest took place in May 1934. The Stalin–Pasternak phone conversation was in June of the same year. Meanwhile, all accounts insist that Mandelstam died a short time after his arrest. They all claim he died in 1938, and always mention his arrest, which means that it is a matter of two arrests, and in no way the same one. So we should more accurately say not 'Mandelstam's arrest' in either 1934 or 1938, but 'one of his arrests', because for all the wonders in the world, it has not yet happened, except perhaps in the Chinese Cultural Revolution, that an arrested person can be arrested again while under arrest. It is like saying that a dead person dies again while dead.

This recycling of time suffices to remind people that after the phone call in 1934 Mandelstam had unexpectedly turned up here and there in public, and once visited Pasternak in Peredel-kino. In short, the poet Mandelstam, in spite of every prediction, had been released after the famous phone call. Some unknown event had intervened, and the sensational phone call had not had its supposed dramatic effect.

An analysis of the locations of the event, the second attribute of any occurrence, shows that something else indeed happened. In a phone conversation, the two speakers are present at the same time, but inevitably in different places. In the case of Stalin and Pasternak, we know that the big chief phoned from the Kremlin, or from one of the locations implied by 'the Kremlin', while the poet replied from his own apartment.

The Kremlin was always unchanging: a building, the state, a symbol. Whereas the poet's apartment was nothing like that.

The phone call in 1934 took place between the Kremlin and Pasternak's apartment on Volkonskaya Street. All accounts agree on this. But between 1934 and 1938, the start and finish of this story, Pasternak moved three times.

Anyone who has lived under the socialist order knows very well that changing your apartment is not simply moving house. In many cases, it's a sign of something else, for good or ill. The first symptom of career advancement, or the opposite, a fall from grace, was the ordinary event of 'moving house'.

Pasternak's apartment on Volkonskaya Street was the most ordinary imaginable for a writer. It was a communal apartment, a *komunalka* as it was called in colloquial Russian, with a corridor, a phone and sometimes a bathroom shared by two or three families.

Not long after the phone call, Pasternak had 'a change of apartment', and not, as might be expected, an unfavourable one. He moved to Lavrushkin Street, to a large building where some of the most famous Moscow writers lived. One imagines that the flats here were of a much higher standard. Moreover, a year later in 1936 he would be given a dacha in famous Peredelkino.

This award made only to distinguished writers was, if not a sign of favour, as least a sure indicator that the phone conversation with Stalin had not done Pasternak the slightest harm.

The mystery surrounding the phone call grew. Perhaps it was an ill-omened phone call, but not in the imagined sense. Perhaps it was prompted by a misinterpretation of the expression 'Kremlin mountaineer', which should have been translated as 'daredevil' of the Kremlin, or even 'hero' of the Kremlin, the sense in which the peoples of the Caucasus refer to the reckless fighters of the mountains.

The latter interpretation is a thread running through history and turns up later, after the fall of communism, in the forthright assertion of a Russian critic, Aleksandr Anaikin, that Stalin was not only not annoyed by the verse, but probably felt honoured by it!

According to Anaikin, weak and complex-ridden school students, such as Stalin, dream of inspiring terror in other people. In other words, hitting out at them and destroying them all. And so, the Russian critic argues, this verse will have given the tyrant a feeling of satisfaction.

However, Anaikin's study fails to explain a contradiction involving the two poets, Mandelstam and Pasternak. Throughout their story, their destiny, with their rise, fall and temporary rise again, followed by their fall again, suggests a connection and mutual dependency. In 1938, fate reserved for Mandelstam a final arrest, followed by death. Pasternak silently followed the tragedy of his counterpart, perhaps expecting similar consequences for himself. But nothing happened, apart from distressing premonitions. Or if something did happen, it was in secret, and nobody found out anything about it.

The suspicions return to the basic fact of the story: the poem. But what if it wasn't that poem that was the cause of everything, including the poet's death? What if it was something else?

It is easy here to imagine a cry of 'enough!'
You're driving us crazy with all these versions!
There's a limit to everything! Enough!
Nevertheless . . .

FIFTH VERSION

'I was having lunch with Pasternak . . .'

Thus starts this version, by the poet's old friend Nikolai Vilmont (*On Pasternak: Memories and Reflections*, Moscow, 1989).

'I remember it was four in the afternoon when the phone rang.'

Vilmont provides other details. A man's voice on the phone: 'Comrade Pasternak, Comrade Stalin wants to speak with you.' Pasternak's reply: 'That's not possible. Don't talk nonsense.' The voice on the phone: 'I repeat, Comrade Stalin wants to speak with you.' The reply: 'Don't play jokes on me.' The voice on the phone: 'I'll give you the phone number. You can call him yourself.' Pasternak turns pale and dials the number.

Another voice on the phone. 'This is Stalin speaking. You're upset [*khlopochete*] about your friend Mandelstam?' Reply: 'We've never been real friends. More the opposite. We have different opinions. But I've always dreamed of talking to you.' Stalin: 'We old Bolsheviks never turned our backs on our friends. And I don't intend to talk to you about nothing.'

'There the conversation was interrupted. Of course, I only heard Pasternak's side, and I couldn't overhear what Stalin said. But these were his words as Boris Leonidovich himself told them to me. Then and there and in full. And immediately afterwards he grabbed the phone again to assure Stalin that Mandelstam really wasn't his friend, and that he hadn't denied a friendship that had never existed out of fear. This explanation seemed necessary to him, more important than anything else.

'There was no reply from the number.'

Sarnov emphasises that Nikolai Vilmont had been one of the people closest to Pasternak in 1934, but says nothing about what this man was like decades later, when he described these events.

It's obvious from the text that Vilmont is not well disposed to his one-time friend. Further questions, however paranoid, are only natural in a totalitarian state. Was he already behaving insincerely towards the poet in 1934, or did he start later? Did the regime turn him that way? And is it therefore a coincidence that he was present at Pasternak's at the exact time when Stalin phoned. Or did he 'turn that way' because of the poison of envy, which can't endure hearing praise for anyone else, even a close friend? Or even attention of an ambivalent kind, the good and the bad, as Pasternak received?

Vilmont is betrayed by the description of what happens after the dictator puts down the phone. According to him, Pasternak reaches for the receiver to remind Stalin that he had never been Mandelstam's friend. However, according to Pasternak and every other account of the incident, he wanted to phone the big boss again for another reason, concerning the misunderstanding over whether he was defending his friend or not. Of course he would have defended his friend, were it not for the confusion of the moment . . . Of course he would, were it not for events . . .

It is entirely plausible that Pasternak would have wanted to say something like that. Firstly, because of the very fact that he mentioned this aspect of the events (his attempt to call back), and secondly because of the lasting anxiety this incident caused him, especially after Mandelstam's death in exile. (He would apparently come to see in everybody's eyes the question of whether he could have saved his friend from this tragedy.) The third and principal reason is his intervention with Stalin one year later to save Anna Akhmatova's second husband and her son Lev Gumilev. In the letter he sent to the dictator in 1935, he mentions Gumilev's criticism of his being 'flustered' (that is for abandoning his friend) the previous year. This time Stalin paid attention. Akhmatova's husband Punin and her son Lev were released one week after the letter, and indeed the leader's same secretary, Poskrebyshev, phoned Pasternak to tell him the good news.

Ultimately there were clear signs of indulgence towards Pasternak. The evidence for this is convincing and easily demonstrable from all accounts, and includes well-known facts such as Pasternak's letter to Stalin, in which he recalls the phone conversation, and is confirmed by personalities such as Anna Akhmatova's son and her second husband.

Yet strangely this evidence has not played the decisive part that it should. The reason must be that this intervention by Stalin was made silently and without any explicit gesture of kindness. Otherwise, the entire case would resonate differently, especially because, of the three main witnesses, Vilmont was the only one not a member of the family.

The second witness was Zinaida Pasternak, the poet's wife, and the third was the poet himself, who, as he admitted, was the cause of the whole mess, indeed its main culprit.

In analysing this mess, it has been suggested that the poet's becoming 'flustered' was the main cause of the confusion. But this discomfiture becomes less significant when it is considered typical of poets.

At first sight, it looks a normal reaction. The country's tyrant phones unexpectedly. Everybody's life and death depended on him. Anyone would have felt a degree of discomfiture.

Pasternak was a distinguished poet. But he was more taken aback than he should have been. When he hears an unknown voice say that Stalin wishes to speak to him, Pasternak feels stunned and awkward. He doesn't want to take this call. He doesn't believe it's real, and in this case disbelief is a form of bewilderment. He thinks someone is trying to make a fool of him. And so there is the second telephone call, and then Stalin's voice.

In his own account of the incident, Pasternak never implies that he didn't want to hear the dictator's voice, for reasons that can be imagined, its rough tone, its dreadful associations. In order to recover the nature of his discomfiture, we must revisit that June afternoon in 1934.

Mandelstam, one of the country's greatest poets, has been arrested. All Moscow is talking about nothing else. With every night that passes and every dawn that breaks, Mandelstam becomes an increasingly frightening and mysterious figure.

Mandelstam has connections with all the well-known poets, including of course Pasternak. Almost all of them can be imagined as a circle of friends, on whom a lightning bolt has just fallen.

Pasternak has reasons to be shaken. Lightning has struck so close to him.

But Pasternak has another, huge reason to be terrified. Two months previously, at a chance meeting in the street, Mandelstam had read out *something* he had written. Pasternak's first thought when he heard Stalin's voice was of *that* . . . Just as it had been when he first heard the news of his friend's arrest. It was *that* . . . just let it not be *that*.

The poem still had no name, which made it even more frightening. As he testified later, Pasternak had not waited for the end before interrupting the author, 'Forget you ever read me that . . . verse. That's not art, it's suicide. I'm not getting involved with it.'

This death knell now had a name, and was called a 'verse'.

Pasternak wasn't the only one to have got upset in this way. Under interrogation, Mandelstam revealed the names of all the people to whom he'd read the verse. He hadn't mentioned Pasternak's name, but Pasternak didn't know this, and still less did Stalin. Indeed, some researchers have thought that the main purpose of the tyrant's phone call was to find out if Pasternak knew the verse or not. Stalin definitely didn't want this verse to get around. Strangely, his anxiety on this point was identical to the poet's.

The verse, as often happens with poems written in anger, was a poor one. Some of its lines were like *stishki*, which could be translated from Russian as 'doggerel' or, more precisely, 'jingles'. Some thought the whole thing was just a provocation.

Not only the portrait of Stalin but everything about it was ill-made and despicable, the style, rhythm and even its use of Russian, so remote from Pushkin:

Kak podkovy kuyot za ukazom ukaz.
Komu v pakh, komu v lob, komu
v brov, komu v glaz.

Like horseshoes his decrees are nailed
On one person's ribs, on another's forehead,
on the brow or eyes.

In these lines, there is someone else present besides the poet. One might say that the poet and the tyrant are together in rapport and at the same time mutual ignorance, as they suspect and fear the same horror.

The laws of tragedy inevitably brought the two of them to this point of contact. Who are you, asking me what I know or don't know?

Sometimes they imagined that they could avoid all this wearisome theatre, but it wasn't possible. The old momentum carried them on. Who are you, who are so frightened of me? And who are you, in yourself? And in the end, who are we all?

Until then, in the poet's eyes the tyrant had been a nothing, an aberration, an eternal negation. Then suddenly something changed. The tyrant's indifference melted away, to be replaced by a covert realisation that the two could understand each other. The question of rank allowed them to accept one another. There was no need for the poet to tell the ruler that he was less than nothing, and not even a proper ruler, while he, the writer, was a genuine ruler and at least knew how to rule properly, alone, and without anybody's help.

Totally exhausted, Pasternak felt the need to retreat into the warmth of his family, where he discovered that there, resting on his wife's breast, the sweetest and most calming words would be the assurance that he had no need to fear the tyrant, because in the end, of the two, he himself was the real *tyranos*, and the other was a mere imitation.

SIXTH VERSION

We are now almost halfway through the versions, and at long last have reached the shelter of the family, who may well take a different view of everything.

Zinaida Nikolayevna Pasternak, the poet's wife, was ill with bronchitis when the incident took place. She herself relates how she was in bed when she heard the phone ringing in the common corridor, and the neighbours running in to say that Boris Leonidovich was being called from the Kremlin. She says that what amazed her most of all was her husband's entirely calm expression.

When I heard him say, 'Hello, Yosif Visarionovich,' the blood went to my head. I could hear only Borya's replies, and was astonished that he spoke to Stalin in the same way as he would talk to me or you.

I realised from the first exchange that it was about Mandelstam. Borya said he was surprised at his arrest, and although there had been no great friendship between them, he valued his writing as the work of a first-rate poet, and always recognised his merits. He asked Stalin to help Mandelstam, and if possible release him. Borya spoke to Stalin plainly and directly, without fine words [*bez ogladok*] or going into politics. I asked Borya how Stalin replied to his suggestion of talking about life and death. It turned out that Stalin said that he would talk with pleasure, but didn't know how to arrange it.

In her testimony, Zinaida emphasises her husband's cool head twice, as one of his qualities, at a time when other people mention his loss of this cool head as a failing.

As for the request for Mandelstam's release, it can be imagined that this is inaccurate, because not even Pasternak himself ever mentions it, or implies such a thing at any time.

As the product of long-term anxiety and an exhausting examination of conscience over something that should have happened but did not, Zinaida Pasternak's evidence is of the sort that, while untrue, still can't be called a lie.

Zinaida had been his wife for a long time. They had been through everything together, doubts, suspicions, anxieties. They had found answers to difficult questions, and tried to find justifications for each other.

However, the sense of distress that Zinaida's evidence conveys goes beyond wifely loyalty. It makes more urgent than ever the question of whether what we know so far is accurate or not.

In her memoirs published in 1993, many years after the event, Zinaida writes that a few hours later all Moscow had found out about the conversation with Stalin.

This detail shows that this positive light, the famous Soviet-style optimism, was not merely a perception confined to the family, but part of the general atmosphere.

Biographers, delving deeper into the married life of the Pasternaks, clearly state that Zinaida did not become 'slightly Soviet' under the pressure of circumstances, but had always been favourably inclined towards the Soviet order.

When writers or artists had problems with the communist state, the married couples or lovers were of two sorts. Some women stoked the discontents of the man they loved, while others tried to calm them. The second group might be motivated by the need to maintain mental balance, and to shield each other from anxiety for their children or fear of exile to remote parts.

There is a final perception of Pasternak as an isolated writer facing the entire Soviet Union, the state and its people. In this context, the relegation of his wife is highly paradoxical. On one hand, she remained his faithful spouse, and on the other, she always belonged to the Soviet Union.

If our poet had been confronted with this interpretation in his lifetime, he would have been put in an awkward position. Ultimately, he might admit that a part of himself remained hostage to his own country, in every sense. His later dilemma, when he had to choose between the Nobel Prize and not being expelled from Russia, apparently shortened his life. But what if the other man, the tyrant, also had his anxieties? They might be of a different order, like everything else connected with a tyrant, but there is no way of not using the same word for them: anxiety.

In their exhausting search for normality or extenuation in their view of the despot, many people remember him walking with his back hunched at his wife's funeral. It's not easy for a dictator who rules one-third of the planet to walk alone behind the coffin of a wife who has killed herself.

In this light, it's natural to ask questions about the phone call to the poet. Why did he make it? Did the ruler really want an explanation about Mandelstam, or was this a mere game?

Then what was this phone call about? What was the reason for it? Was it really about some verses? Or something similar? As has been rumoured recently, it was indeed about a poem but not the one we know. Perhaps an ode . . . ?

SEVENTH VERSION

Nadya sent a telegram to the Central Committee, and Stalin gave an order for the matter to be looked into . . . Then he phoned Pasternak. What followed after is very well known . . . Stalin reported that instructions had been given for everything to be straight regarding Mandelstam. He asked Pasternak why he hadn't intervened [*blopotal*].

(These apparently ordinary words come

from the diary of Anna Akhmatova, the most
famous of all the witnesses.)

Something striking might have been expected
from the great lady of Russian–Soviet literature
in the twentieth century. But perhaps because
this was what she was, at a distance and remote
from what was happening around her, her testimony is at first sight disappointing.

Akhmatova was the most mythologised writer
of her times. She earned particular fame thanks
to her unforgettable silhouette drawn by Amedeo Modigliani in a Paris café. She married very
young, to the famous acmeist poet Gumilev, and
after her husband was shot led a troubled life in
Russia, the like of which few experienced.

Always poised between fame and disaster,
beautiful, capricious, 'the queen of the Neva'
according to her admirers, and 'half nun, half
whore' according to Andrey Zhdanov, called by
some 'the Sappho of Russia', or 'Anna of all the

Russias', in the monarchist–imperial style of one young poet, she was also acquainted with Mandelstam and Pasternak, the two leading poets of the time.

She and Pasternak had dedicated not entirely innocent verses to each other, to the point where Pasternak, whenever he chanced to meet her, would forget that she had a husband and would propose marriage to her, which she just as naturally refused.

Again in her diary, on 8 July 1963, three years before her death, she writes of both of them:

Nadya [i.e. Nadezhda Mandelştam, the arrested poet's wife] sent a telegram . . .

Later, Akhmatova relates the conversation between the tyrant and the poet.

'If a poet friend of mine were to go to prison, I would move heaven and earth to save him.'

Pasternak replied that if he'd intervened [*blopotal*], Stalin wouldn't have agreed.

'But he's your friend?' Pasternak shrivelled! After a silence, Stalin went on to ask, 'But he's a great poet, isn't he?' Pasternak replied, 'That isn't so important.'

B.L. [Boris Leonidovich] thought that Stalin wanted to find out if he knew about Mandelstam's poem or not, and he had replied evasively because of this.

'Why are we talking about Mandelstam, when I've wanted for so long to talk with you?'

'What about?'

'About life, about death.'

Stalin put down the phone.

As in every version, there are contradictions in this one too, although it comes from a person of great stature. The first question is whether Akhmatova heard the conversation directly or from someone else.

One thinks first of the poet's wife Nadya Mandelstam who had been her close friend for many years. Probably the spirit of faint hope that protracted despair creates belonged more to the wife of the martyred poet than to Akhmatova.

Anna describes this incident in her diary as if it were a storm, or more accurately two storms which, although long past, came together.

The entry of these women into what might today be called the Stalin–Pasternak case was welcomed with both hope and despair, that is with as much joy as fear.

This happened especially in cases where there were suspicions and inexplicable riddles. Women appeared from unexpected directions, from across borders and in remote languages, and sometimes from beyond the grave.

As has often been said, Boris Pasternak was still alive when speculation began about which woman was hidden behind the character of Lara Antipova in the novel *Doctor Zhivago*. Was it his wife Zinaida Nikolayevna, or his lover Olga Ivinskaya? After his death, the rivalry between the two, which should have been easy to settle, grew to the point of preoccupying the entire world.

It was a recurring ritual. At first it seemed obvious that his lover should be the woman described in the novel, that is the woman doctor, and yet the day came when his wife seemed to occupy this place, and her claim was hard to refute.

After the poet's death, when both were still alive, a third rival appeared silently, delicately, with almost ghostly steps.

Such interventions are rare in poets' biographies. It was so surprising that it might be called an intervention of the people, in the teeth of the claims of critics and chroniclers. It seemed that the people could change something that seemed fixed, although it would take a very long time.

The third woman who became close to Boris

Pasternak was Anna Akhmatova. There had indeed been rumours of this sort, but they were impossible to credit, and so were dismissed for want of evidence.

As time passed, the speculations revived, especially after Pasternak's death and the deaths of the three women. Now that it was a time of ghosts, everything seemed to fall into place more easily.

Sometimes it seemed simple: the Russian people, like others who loved literature, liked to find suitable brides for the poets they loved. In other words, to make and break marriages, even though they took place out of time and against all logic.

The first rumours of an engagement between Boris Pasternak and Anna Akhmatova might have circulated for a hundred years, and no wonder, given that they would be married for a thousand years.

For example, the present writer heard them for

the first time about half a century after leaving
Moscow, in 2010. I had returned for the first
time to the city where I had been a student, this
time not in a dream but in reality. I'm really
going back, I thought as I glanced at the Paris–
Moscow plane ticket, as if to persuade myself
that an actual plane was taking me there and not
a tram with horns, as had appeared in a dream
recently, not to mention those two astonishing
creatures, half prostitutes, half lightning flashes,
whom I had begged to give me a lift as a hitch-
hiker one month ago.

You can imagine what my first day in Moscow
was like after half a century. And especially the
night. Some time past midnight, channel-
hopping, I settled at last on a film that seemed to
me more or less normal: pretty women, luxurious surroundings, Russian production.

Perhaps I wouldn't have noticed the name
'Anna' of one of the characters had there not
been a mention in the film of a forbidden book.

As they spoke, the eyes of the author of this book too melted as the woman's gaze become more tender and beautiful.

But this is Anna with Boris Pasternak, I thought. I had heard things, but only obscurely, about a possible flirtation between the two. But on the screen they were very close, almost lovers, though not engaged.

The next day I asked my Russian escort if anything of this kind had been discovered when the archives were opened, but he paid little attention. People say all sorts of things about everybody, he said.

The conversation led to Stalin's phone call, about which my escort had clearer knowledge. Apparently, it had actually happened, just as described. When I told him I was writing something about this phone call, he said, 'Really? How wonderful!'

I wanted to revert to the topic of the possible Anna–Boris flirtation, especially why the popular matchmakers had been so slow on the uptake, but something prevented me, perhaps not taking my Russian escort for a 'matchmaker'.

EIGHTH VERSION

Although this version again starts with the name of Nadya, the poet's wife Nadezhda Mandelstam, this is the most sparse, not to say bleakest, account of the events.

This is to some extent understandable. If any version of this entire story might be shot through with an element of anxiety, bad conscience and regret, it would be hers.

Stalin began by telling Pasternak that Mandelstam's case had been reviewed, and everything would be all right. This was followed by a strange reproach: why hadn't Pasternak approached the writers' organisations or "him personally" and why hadn't he tried to do something for Mandelstam?

Like in Akhmatova's short description, Nadezhda Mandelstam's narrative starts with Stalin's hopeful words, which means that he didn't phone Pasternak to seek his advice at all about whether to punish or forgive the troublesome (*opalniy*) poet, but about something else.

What that 'something else' might be seems a question especially for enquiries of this kind.

An impartial assessment of the evidence shows that the communication consists of two themes. The first contains information, news about a matter which is making good progress. The second part is an angry reproach about the same question.

At first sight the two themes, the good news and the reproach, appear contradictory. But a closer examination shows them not only to be compatible but to support each other.

Pasternak emerges relieved from both. Stalin is clearly giving him good news about his imprisoned friend. The reproach only reinforces the idea that it is good news.

Meanwhile, it isn't hard to discern a coldness towards Pasternak in the memoirs of Osip Mandelstam's widow Nadya. This is an incidental misunderstanding, a sensitivity that arose later on towards her husband's friend, colleague and rival, a man who was fortunate in everything, while her own husband was fortunate in nothing.

Nadezhda Mandelstam's famous memoirs, or rather her coldness, could be decisive in establishing the muted confrontation between the two geniuses.

Did later events cast light on this mystery, or did she herself, as the person closest to the poet, know secrets hidden from everybody else?

Her summons to the Lubyanka, where her husband had been confined, to be asked by an interrogator if she wanted to accompany him into exile or not, is one of the most tragic scenes in this story. We know nothing about how the meeting between her and her husband went apart from her agreement to go with him. We know nothing about how the meeting between them went, what they said to each other, their glances or her doubts, if she had any. Above all we don't know the purpose of this grim theatre, overheard no doubt by many investigators, some present and some in secret. Of course we also don't know what might have happened offstage – perhaps promises were given, directly or indirectly.

The search of Mandelstam's house during the arrest or immediately afterwards was no less grim. According to Anna Akhmatova, the secret police agents roughly grabbed the poet's manuscripts. This combination of eagerness and carelessness was seen later as proof that they were looking for something highly specific: the manuscript of a poem.

The feverish scene recalls a similar one, almost

a hundred years previously, when the seriously wounded Pushkin was languishing in the drawing room of his house, and the tsar's police, with the same rough impatience, came looking for the manuscript of the poem *'Exegi monumentum'*. But in Mandelstam's case it was the expression 'Kremlin mountaineer', which they didn't know if they would find in a manuscript or not. In Pushkin's case, the manuscript of the poem was known to exist, but the concern was about a single word in it.

So much has been said about this search of Pushkin's house, whose purpose was not to destroy this testamentary poem but simply to erase the word 'Aleksandr'. It was a single word, but it was the name of the Russian tsar of the time, and thus a very delicate matter. This explains the participation in the search of Vasily Zhukovsky, the foremost Russian poet of the time. Zhukovsky, as 'literary supervisor of the search', a newly created profession, was the sole person authorised to change the text or, if that was impossible, destroy it entirely.

It seems that Zhukovsky enjoyed the tsar's trust, but the poet's even more. He was pained by what would be done to Pushkin's well-known poem, and so quickly, to rescue it, he changed the dangerous word, perhaps then and there during the confusion of the search. He replaced the name of Aleksandr with Napoleon. And so, when the two monumental columns mentioned in the poem are compared in height, the poet's is compared not to the Russian tsar's but to the French emperor's.

Pushkin doesn't despise 'the column of the tsar'. He simply writes that the poet's column, that is his own, was 'built taller [*vyshe*] than Aleksandr's column'.

Zhukovsky is careful in his amendment. He doesn't go into trivialities such as which of the two columns is taller, the poet's or the tsar's. He hits upon another emperor to displace the contest to a distant country, to France. And he succeeds: his repair work does its job, rescuing the poem from this first and most dangerous furore.

Zhukovsky's change didn't survive long, but simply vanished, without any intervention, by France for instance, to replace Napoleon's column with a different one, say British or Turkish. This was for the simple reason that several copies of the original manuscript had survived during the poet's lifetime.

There is no comparison between the two searches' dramatic character and still less between their consequences. The replacement of a single word was sufficient to save Pushkin's testament, but in Mandelstam's case much more was required than the destruction of the manuscript. Its very memory had to be erased, and the manner of its erasure.

Are we exaggerating in this description of the grotesque nature of the times?

Meanwhile, things believable only in books

and never in real life were giving way to things in real life that would not be believed in books.

We see a lane in the writers' village of Peredelkino where two poets are talking as they walk. These two aren't Isakovsky and Isaak Babel, nor Fadayev and Pavlenko, but those inseparable opposites Pasternak and Mandelstam. And this is the year 1937. Are we seeing ghosts?

For it really is 1937, three years after the unforgettable year 1934 in which terrifying things had happened: the phone call, Mandelstam's arrest and exile, and his attempted suicide. After three years all these things are only dimly remembered, like a long-closed chapter.

Surely these two scenes can't both be true. Either we're dealing with the drama of June 1934 and all its consequences, or that drama was a sick fantasy at a time when the real truth is here in Peredelkino, where the two poets are taking a walk, as poets might do anywhere in the world.

A true account of this whole story includes

both these scenes. The terrors that Mandelstam underwent have been shown to be true, and even the floor and window of the building from which the poet threw himself in 1934 have been identified, just as we know his places of internment and the hut where he died unnoticed. Yet just as precisely, if not more so, we have evidence for the second scene, the happy one, of Mandelstam's arrival as a guest at the villa of his friend Pasternak in Peredelkino!

So both events must be accepted, and are confirmed simultaneously by rumours, newspaper reports, files of the secret police, contemporary and modern Western researchers, without any suggestion that one might be a dream and the other real.

And so these ghosts walked in Peredelkino in 1937, talking and reading each other the occasional poem.

The same scene, with two different interpretations or two scenes with the same interpretation?

And then that poem crops up again. Perhaps in the happy scene, perhaps in the other. There have been plenty of rumours of another poem, of an opposite character to the first, indeed obviously so, as is evident in the title: 'Ode to Stalin'.

This is another outrage to the imagination. If this poem existed, why didn't Pasternak rush to the phone to report the news? Perhaps no phone line in the world existed that could carry the news that Osip M. had at last written the required poem, an unbelievable one. But the shock might lead to one being specially created.

This is a mere if . . .

People had every right to be confused. The signs of the times were impossible to interpret, often having two meanings, and sometimes three.

For years, students mulled over those three minutes in that distant summer of 1934, but without result. Histories were pored over, and the different versions examined. In 2014 the Israeli press commemorated the eightieth anniversary of the famous phone call. Soon it will be a century, and still there will be no clear settlement.

There were further mysteries. Mandelstam's many arrests were remembered, but not his releases, to the point that people suspected that the real reason for each release was his imminent rearrest.

Other conundrums unexpectedly changed the meaning of events. It was in the summer of 1934, only a few days after the three-minute phone call, at a time when Pasternak's arrest was expected, that to everyone's disbelief he chaired a session at the formal congress of the Writers' Union, which loudly proclaimed Soviet socialist realism to the world.

The question of the poems about Stalin remained inscrutable. There were continual rumours of two poems, the 'bad one' about the mountaineer, which dug a pit for the poet, and the other, the 'good' one, the ode, which did not rescue him from it.

When two people talked about these poems, usually in low voices, a moment would come when their eyes would avoid each other. There was something about the story which wasn't right, but which couldn't be said openly. Because one of the poems was deadly and the other not, it must have been the ode that was written first, and the fatal poem after it.

Yet the opposite was true. All the information showed that the 'mountaineer' poem came first, and that this poem alone was the reason for the phone call.

This sort of conversation generally ended in silence, sometimes with an exhausted sigh suggesting regret at getting mixed up in such a tangle.

There were rumours of a photograph from the last days of Lenin's life, in which symptoms of syphilis were clearly visible. Incredibly, our classmate Stulpans brought a copy of this photo from Riga. I had never seen anything so sad.

'This explains everything,' he said. I said I was surprised that the photo hadn't been destroyed. Stulpans smiled. He'd said the same to his friend, who had replied that not only would it not be destroyed, but he was sure it would be closely cherished. His explanation was very strange. He said that this photograph not only did Lenin no harm, but being the only picture which showed a human side to this supernatural being, it would probably be used in the future as the sole piece of evidence in his favour.

I gasped.

'You may think that is going too far,' he said to me in a low voice. That is what he himself had first thought. But his friend had explained that a time would come when every horror would be laid bare. Marx's turn as well, he added.

Marx too?

We stared at each other in silence.

Instead of continuing with Marx, he asked me what little bird had suggested to Albania that it should become the Soviet Union's closest ally, for it was 2,000 kilometres away, unlike Latvia, which was next door.

I shrugged my shoulders, not knowing what to say. He sensed that the subject irritated me, as it did whenever the subject of the servility of small allies like Albania towards Russia was broached, even indirectly. It seemed to me deeply humiliating and Stulpans couldn't say he didn't know this, and so, to mollify me, he admitted that Latvia was in the same position.

Stulpans listened to me thoughtfully as I told him that, if it was a question of fascism and Nazism, Albania in no sense lagged behind compared to the other countries in the family.

Fascist Albania, he whispered. While studying Migjeni, he had gained a sense of such a thing, but strangely this expression was never used, or only rarely.

I said that he was quite right, and even I, as I
pronounced the words 'fascist Albania', felt that
my mouth was unused to them. They aren't
uttered openly even today, but I couldn't understand why, perhaps because of the ambiguous
relationships between the Albanian fascists,
nationalists and communists. There was the
well-known whispered story about how the communists didn't get on badly with the Nazis to
start with, but declared war on them on the day
the latter attacked the Soviet Union. And then
there was the typically Albanian story of the
nationalists joining forces with the Germans to
spite the communists, because, being unable to
tolerate the idea of collective farms, they claimed
that this what the national interest called for.

Stulpans didn't take his eyes off me as he listened. Maybe he thought that I was going too
far, and I became almost tetchy with him: if I
believed this stuff about Lenin's syphilis, he
should also believe my own exaggerations.

Reading my mind, he reverted unexpectedly to Lenin. He said that he too had argued against his friend about the Russian leader's venereal disease, which despite its ugly reputation was nothing more than a disease, and so something human.

I recognised his gentler tone that invariably led to justifications of the savagery of the times. But Stulpans was more annoyed than usual. According to him, Lenin had exceeded all bounds. Stulpans was referring to the murder of the tsar's family. When the monarchy was destroyed, everything and everybody went with it, emperor, empress, the little princes and princesses. Everybody knew this, but there was worse.

'What do you mean, there was worse?' I asked.

'There is always worse,' he said. 'Another time I'll tell you things that beggar belief. I'll show you what this Lenin of ours was like.'

Stulpans' voice was about to crack. 'Listen,' he went on. 'I talk like this because it's painful to me. You should know everything this man did to my Latvia . . . and your Albania, surely.'

His speech was becoming increasingly confused. Perhaps sensing this, and to make himself clearer, he inserted the occasional Albanian word, while I reflected that I was destined to suffer this final torture, never before experienced on this earth, of hearing the story of a Latvian in Russian, mixed with seventeenth-century Albanian.

He was trying to explain that although he seemed to totally despair of the present day, in fact he was trying to make our own times easier to accept. 'I think you must have felt the same,' he said, '*hast thou not*? We have wanted not to be ashamed of our times, because after all we have suffered because of them. *What thinkest thou?*'

'You imagine there can have been nothing worse than the shooting of the princesses? What did the Russian leader do with the reports coming to him from distant provinces, on whose basis he was supposed to make decisions to improve the Russian people's situation? He would leaf through the lists, and next to the name of each province note the urgent measures to be taken to save people from cold and hunger. His aides looked on, amazed that this genius could identify an instant solution in every case. In Voronezh, an 11 per cent increase in the number of extra-judicial killings would suffice, although that wouldn't be necessary in Chelyabinsk. But in Ekaterinburg, always a nest of anti-Soviet activity, even 23 per cent would not be enough. And so, with a father's care, he would work out what figure was appropriate for each region, from Krasnoyarsk, for example, to Novosibirsk and as far as Samarkand and Gropa e Qyqes. Twelve per cent . . . Does that seem tolerable to you? There's more to come. All these figures and percentages passed through Lenin's own hands, sometimes with an affectionate sigh, as if they were the love letters that he had never managed to write.

'And so it came to the imperial family. This was a question that had loomed since the first moments of the revolution. What would happen to them?

'Their destruction, of course, had been inevitable since the fall of the monarchy, and was necessarily signed by Lenin's own hand. And then came the princesses' turn. Millions of little girls would have liked to be caressed with that name as they combed their hair in front of their mirrors.

'Of all the billions of words created in all the languages of the world, there could be none sweeter or more innocent. But this didn't stay Lenin's hand. He had persuaded himself that he wouldn't be held back by anything, and certainly not these sirens with enchanting names. And so he signed their death sentence.

'And last of all, though no less important, the tsarevich, the emperor's son, his heir, who would assume the throne, and lose it. He was the ultimate target of every regicide.

'Hundreds of monarchs have been overthrown, and the eyes and ears of the world have become inured even to the most horrific cases, the slaughter of crowned infants. But don't say this is all familiar knowledge. Lenin's hand reached out to sign the death of someone both known and unknown, the haemophiliac tsarevich. This was a special kind of murder. The merest scratch is enough to kill any haemophiliac, and Lenin knew this. But he had no compunction about ordering the firing of countless machine-gun bullets that would cause thousands of deaths as well as that of the child-tsar.

'And I imagine how this man, now at the summit of power, had been on some dark alley in Zurich a few years before, face to face with some tiny prostitute, this ordinary, timid little man with a few words of German: "What's your price, girl?" Disgusting isn't it? Yet this jerk with thinning hair, in this sole moment where he shows some humanity, when a little European whore is about to share her syphilis, seems an angel compared to that repellent leader of Russia with his percentages.

> ' "Little whore, you came too late.
> Too late by several years." '

I was stunned and couldn't grasp what he meant.

Stulpans continued to stare at me. How could this Zurich whore have been too late, what mistake could she have made, as she transferred syphilis through her tender loins?

'Nobody could have known, and she possibly never knew herself. And so she departed this world, wounding the monster, but not killing him.'

Stulpans apologised for his wild speech, while I thought back to Marx, or more precisely to his illness, which must have been even more ghastly than Lenin's, but Stulpans looked so overcome that I didn't dare mention it.

Marx's turn will come, I thought again, as I tried to follow Stulpans' muttering. 'Three minutes,' he said, 'just three minutes and we've almost gone out of our minds analysing them, then just imagine this whole epoch, the most perfidious in history. And you thought that seven versions might be too many. There could never be too many. Too few, certainly.'

He repeated what he had said in even more archaic Albanian, perhaps of the sixteenth century, from which he had translated a psalm.

'And the riddle could be solved from the tiniest detail of these stories. Do you remember the day when we talked about the sphinx?'

'No,' I hastily replied.

'I understand. You're tired. We're all tired.'

'Yosif Sifilisovich Stalin,' he said. Then he talked again about those times. He had read a poem by Anna Akhmatova in which she mentioned the apocalypse and the words of an angel, saying 'there will be no more time'.

Are you going to say we need to hurry? I thought.

He said something I couldn't understand at all, and added that Anna had said she had written some of her poems from the 1940s while dead.

I had heard this, but still I said it was impossible.

'Impossible,' he repeated.

We had been using this word increasingly often, as if to tell ourselves that something impossible was really happening between us.

Were we now becoming impossible to each other?

As the years passed we shared less of ourselves.

But our conversations continued in my mind. Stulpans, you were my closest friend on the course. But there is no need to pretend to be dead. Because that is what you really are.

Stulpans killed himself a long time ago, after my departure from Moscow. But still I continued my unfinished conversations with him, especially about the possible quarrel between Albania and the Soviet Union. Was it really a quarrel or a game? Or something else? Would we really not see each other ever again, or just pretend?

The most incredible thing had happened. In the Soviet press, as well as the Latvian, Albania was now called fascist. Perhaps the time would come when Latvia would be called the same. Meanwhile, Stulpans was no more. And I was still here.

Little Jeronim Stulpans, deceased.

Whether I wished to or not, I would also endure that frightening journey through light and darkness, intermingled as in all great misunderstandings.

I often thought that Pasternak's three minutes were one of my overworked obsessions, of which I would do well to rid myself. And at other times it seemed different.

Whether by accident or not, this phone call was so close to me, and I was compelled to analyse each moment of those fatal 200 seconds, when the laws of tragedy had brought the poet and the tyrant together.

It was a grim collision, which should not have taken place, and yet it did, to our fellow artist's misfortune.

And so, we who know something about this matter are obliged to bear witness to it, even those aspects that are impossible to confirm. Moment by moment, second by second . . . Just as he and all our brothers-in-art bore witness to it, without anybody knowing and without taking anyone's side. Because art, unlike a tyrant, receives no mercy, but only gives it.

NINTH VERSION

And so moment by moment, impartially and pitilessly, the ninth version: the year is 1934. Nobody has cast any doubt on it. The witness: a woman, the sixth so far.

Of the thirteen versions, the majority are from women.

The first testimony, which was long suspected to be a KGB fiction, was that of the actor Zinaida Antonova, someone later forgotten. The second version was again connected to a woman, and the main thing that will be remembered from it is the name of Tchaikovsky, whose niece she was.

Speculation on any event focuses on women, as both the sweetest and the most ruthless explainers of the inexplicable. So it has been since Helen of Troy.

It was little children who first asked who the woman was with that name. Later there was nobody who didn't know that she had the most famous love story of all the billions of women on this planet.

This was easy to say, but not easy to understand, and still harder to make credible.

The Homeric poems and later the classical tragedies insisted on this, even if only casually, as often happens with things that are well known. In their long processions of thousands with their war chariots and murdered kings, the story of Helena is occasionally mentioned as the greatest scandal of the age.

The need to shed light on the planet's secrets was as hard to resist as it was to respond to. There were times when people thought that the world in which they lived had so many mysteries that it would have no room to hold any more.

Helen of Troy, a woman who had left her husband's home with her lover, to return to her husband twenty years later, became fixed in the world's mind not as a 'loyal wife' but as a 'faithless woman', whose loyalty was to life itself (or to socialist realism, as Zhdanov would say).

Logic would demand that, after the sensational scandal, she could have earned different sobriquets from the two warring peoples, 'Helen of Troy' from the Greeks and 'Helen of Greece' from the Trojans. Each people being inclined to link her disastrous name with their enemies. Later when the fortunes of war changed and the Trojans were defeated, their name for her, Helen of Greece, fell into disuse and she was left for ever with the name by which we know her now, Helen of Troy.

This bride of death, who bore the name of the city that was destroyed because of her, even after her return to her husband, has provoked millions of words and reflections.

In spite of this river of speculation, she herself remains almost totally silent. We don't hear even her most ordinary exclamations: take me. Leave me. Carry me to Troy. Anywhere but there. Take me back to Greece. Anywhere but there.

We know nothing of any of these, just as we don't know whether we should respect this woman's silence, or keep asking her questions. About the famous abduction, if it really happened; about the long journey (did those walls over there belong to Troy?), and many other things, apart from the graves of the dead soldiers, which are usually neither looked for nor pointed out.

We still don't know anything about that little nine-year-old girl from Florence, a certain Beatrice Portinari, whose eyes twenty centuries later met a boy's by the church door. And nine years later she chanced to smile at the same boy, without knowing his name. Then nothing. And after that everything.

They would never see each other again, and of course never touch. They would marry other people, and produce children, and die. But the secret of the divine poem that they wove together, some place created out of nowhere, where nobody is born or dies, cannot be known.

Three centuries later, someone might chance upon a third woman, to continue this impossible conversation. She has a beautiful name, Dulcinea the sweet lady of Toboso. Now it's her turn to say, I don't know anything, or understand anything. Because unlike other women I am lodged in the mind of a man who is mad. Nevertheless, you two, yourself and this madman, have created a jewel for humankind. Do you understand, lady? No I don't. We never touched one another. That doesn't matter. You are in his mind. But he is out of his mind, sir. I am in this story for no reason. I am, as you might say, there by accident . . . in a delusion.

It has been true for centuries that a clear head, or in other words reason, and its opposite, the absence of reason, find it hard to live together. However, there have been times when the absence of reason is preferred above all else, especially in love and art. The word 'mystery' does not worry many women, especially the many who like riddles. Such women can turn an early autumn cold that changes their voice and breath, or a weakness of eyesight, into ploys of enticement. And so they turn natural states into a new form of awareness, which Russian writers called 'a state of love', following the example of the French expression 'l'état d'amour' on the model of 'l'état de guerre'.

Women of this kind may be good for many things, but not as witnesses. A genuine, cool-headed and uninvolved witness, if she were to feel a weakness in her eyesight, would not use this failing eyesight to make coy glances but would hurry to the optician to order suitable spectacles. The sixth female witness, who did not belong to any of the well-known cliques of 'enigmatic women', was Maria Pavlovna Bogoslovskaya, the wife of Sergey Bobrov, a futurist poet of the time, known to the reader from the third version in these pages.

She entrusted her story to Viktor Duvakin, the same person who tape-recorded her husband's account of the incident.

Here is the text:

'As soon as I returned to Moscow from my place of internment, I wanted to do something for my husband. Something to help, such as gaining permission for a publication. In short, I went to Pasternak. At first the conversation revolved around Sergey Pavlovich [her husband] and what could be done to help him. Pasternak's face clouded, and he said that he was unable to do anything. Did I know about his conversation with Stalin?

'No, I didn't. He told me everything, and added, "It wasn't easy for me to talk. I had people in the house."

'Stalin had asked him what he thought about Mandelstam. "And here you see the poet's sincerity and honesty," Pasternak said to me. "I can't talk about something I don't feel. It would be foreign to me. That's what I said to him, that I couldn't say anything about Mandelstam."'

'Does that mean that Pasternak didn't say Mandelstam was a great poet?'

'He said nothing. That's what he told me

himself, that he said nothing. And he justi-
fied himself, saying he couldn't betray
himself.'

'And why did he mention this matter?'

'I had recited to him some lines of Sergey
Pavlovich [Bobrov]. He said that these were
not among the lines of Bobrov that he liked.
Besides this, there was nothing in his power
that he could do . . . You understand, after
this conversation, my prestige [*moy prestizh*]
has sunk.'

(Text according to *Osip and Nadezhda
Mandelstam*, Moscow, 2002.)

In the first part of the narrative Maria Bogoslovskaya repeats a familiar ritual of Russian wives:
they leave their husbands in their place of internment, come to Moscow and cross and recross the
city to look for help. It seems entirely credible.
She meets Pasternak and the first part of their
conversation also sounds believable, until the

moment when 'his face clouded' and he says to her that there's no way he can help.

This is the moment when something breaks down between them. We don't know if Pasternak fell silent for a moment. Nor do we know anything more about the situation that now arose between them. Pasternak might have questioned his own sincerity. It was something he rightly asked of himself, but were other people sincere with him?

Pasternak's naivety was famous. Yet even he would have grasped that the simple, impartial, naive Maria Bogoslovskaya was not being sincere.

Perhaps he had an inkling but had suppressed it out of respect for his interned colleague. He asks, 'Do you know about my conversation with Stalin?' But might have said, 'You no doubt know about my conversation with Stalin?' She makes the outrageous reply, 'No.' Pasternak again restrains himself. Instead of saying, madam, you travelled two thousand kilometres to tell me this fib? How come you don't know what all Moscow has been talking about for months on end? Or if you haven't heard, then what about your husband Bobrov, whose eye nothing escapes, hasn't he told you?

Pasternak then did something inconceivable. He related to the simple Maria the most diabolical conversation of his life, without avoiding its dangerous import. Did he do this in order not to let himself down, as he says, or out of respect for his colleague? In either case, his sincerity remains beyond reproach.

In order to understand more, we must go back to the third version, one of the basic accounts, told by Sergey Bobrov himself.

The conversation took place between Sergey Bobrov and Viktor Duvakin, the critic and professor of literature who was present at all the events of this time.

Bobrov and Duvakin are alone after the

Moscow summer of 1934, after Mandelstam's arrest and certainly after Stalin's phone call.

Bobrov starts the conversation.

'Did you hear that Borya Pasternak refused to help Mandelstam?'

Bobrov doesn't wait for the other man's reply but, as if to muster courage, says that he has heard this story twice.

There are some surprising features from the very start of this conversation. The first unexpected thing is that Bobrov knows something that Duvakin seems not to know. (Both are members of Pasternak's circle and there is no evidence anywhere that Bobrov is closer to him than the other man, which would explain the above.) The second surprise is that Bobrov is not only aware of this 'something' but, in emphasising this fact, hastens to say that he has heard this story twice, and on one of these occasions from his wife (the simple, marginalised Maria). In this case his superiority over Duvakin (if knowledge of Pasternak's affairs can be taken as a sign of superiority) is evident.

Duvakin's reply is the greatest surprise in this dialogue. Unlike Pasternak, Duvakin isn't naive and he knows how to draw conclusions. His answer pours cold water on Bobrov. He not only knows what has happened to Pasternak, but in contrast to Bobrov, who heard it from his wife, he, Duvakin, heard everything from the mouth of Pasternak himself.

Duvakin doesn't stop at this. He's no defender of Pasternak, and he even admits his colleague's mistake, but nevertheless, when faced with Bobrov's cynicism, without hiding his annoyance, he asks: but where did you hear this news? (This rubbish, these tales?) From Pasternak himself, like me, or from someone else? (Shklovsky, for instance.)

Sergey Bobrov must have felt in a tight spot as seldom before in his life. This whole conversation is laden with questions that are impossible to answer. The first and most important, when did this 'event' take place? Before Bobrov's internment? During it, or after it?

No less painful is the question of why this happened. There are several kinds of why, each harder than the last. There is the question of why Bobrov told Duvakin. Other questions, such as the real reason why he sent his wife to Pasternak, are no less fraught.

So, when and why?

Rarely can a when and why have been so inseparable. One of the most recent publications of the tape-recorded conversation is from 2002, when all the participants were dead. Sergey Bobrov died in 1971, and so this conversation with Duvakin must have taken place between 1934 and 1971. Thirty-seven years is a very long time over which to remember such a brief event. This stretch of time includes the Scandinavian year of 1958. Many people have looked for everything in that fatal year. They looked to this year to solve the mystery of the phone call, even though it took place a quarter of acentury earlier.

One can imagine the arrival of Maria, Sergey Dobrov's wife, at her place of internment, where her husband was serving his sentence, like Mandelstam before him.

Arriving in this alien landscape was a well-known ritual for Russian wives. This place was now 'his' home. Tears on cheeks, and a first few moments of silence, until the husband's question, 'What's happening back in Moscow?'

The answer to this question was both difficult and unnecessary, to the point where a shrug of the shoulders sufficed. What's happening? We all know. There is less of everything, starting with phone calls. And then the other things can be imagined. Friends, acquaintances being taken away, better not to ask . . . However, of course the husband asked and the wife answered, and the conversation finally took place. Any news of Mandelstam? And what about the two ladies, apart from the rumour that one of them tried to hang herself, which was fortunately not true. Which of the two? he asked. I don't think it would be Anna. That's what I thought, it would be the other one, Tsvetaeva. He asked about Pasternak, but her reply was unclear. Maria shrugged her shoulders again. She expected his perpetual reproaches for her inability to understand the latest news, but surprisingly he said something else. He looked at her closely. 'Listen,' he said. He started to explain something in a slow voice. She interrupted him to say there was no reason for him to stare at her like that. She knew Pasternak, and so there was no reason why she shouldn't visit him the day after tomorrow, when she got back to Moscow. Like all wives with interned husbands . . . and there was no reason to ask why, everybody knew.

But the why in this case is less obvious. Why did Bobrov send his wife to Pasternak? Did Bobrov really believe that Pasternak would do for him what he hadn't done for his own friend Mandelstam? And finally, did he think that Stalin would heed his intervention? It's unlikely that Bobrov himself had any hope of this. Then the question of why would come in its own time. It surfaced at the very start of the story, and then later, always, like a tolling bell, down to the present day.

All these ramifications of the evidence of the minor figure of this naive woman show that the enigmas of communism crop up where you least expect them. Sons denounce their fathers. Grandmothers grandsons. A government minister denounces his tailor. Clichés collapse more quickly than at any other time, especially clichés connected to women.

So what to do? Abandon them as soon as the situation becomes more complicated, as in the Pasternak case?

No way.

TENTH VERSION

Olga Ivinskaya, Pasternak's lover, occupied a privileged position due to her rivalry with his wife, Zinaida Pasternak, but even more so in the celestial regions of art. The dispute over which of the two is the character of Lara in *Doctor Zhivago* was so widespread that mentioning it was a sign less of culture than of philistinism.

Complications of the wife/lover sort, according to the long-standing cliché, are generally solved in favour of the lover. In the Pasternak case, it doesn't work out so clearly. One's impression is that the poet himself, in the role of arbiter, becomes more confused than in the conversation with Stalin.

When the thunderbolt struck [i.e. when the telephone rang] from the Kremlin with the words, 'Comrade Stalin wants to speak with you,' B.L. [Boris Leonidovich] was rendered almost mute.

This the first testimony to the incident which Olga Ivinskaya gives, as she heard of it from other people, mainly from Pasternak himself. According to her:

The leader spoke in a rough [*grubovato*] voice, using *ti* as he usually did. 'Tell me, what's the gossip in your literary circles about Mandelstam's arrest?'

B.L., wrapping up concrete facts in philosophical arguments as usual, replied, 'You know, there is no gossip, because to have gossip you have to have literary circles. But there are no literary circles because everyone is scared.'

A long silence on the phone, and then, 'All right, then tell me your personal opinion about Mandelstam. What do you think about this poet?'

And here B.L., with his characteristic vacillation, said that he and Mandelstam were poets going in totally different directions.

When B.L. stopped talking, Stalin, in a tone of contempt, said, 'So you don't know how to stand up for your friend,' and put down the phone.

B.L. told me that at that moment he froze completely. Stalin had hung up in such an insulting fashion, in a way he thought he had deserved.

(Olga Ivinskaya, *A Captive of Time: My Years with Pasternak*, Moscow, 1972.)

Benedikt Sarnov draws attention to Stalin's use of the intimate *ti* and for this reason thinks that this story is not a product of Ivinskaya's imagination. This is the only testimony that supplies this detail. Of the two possible explanations, that the use of *ti* is a sign of intimacy or a sign of contempt on the part of the boorish tyrant, Ivinskaya chooses the latter.

Pasternak himself never mentions this point,

either because it escaped his notice in his state of shock, or because he doesn't wish to recall it, as happens with exceptionally hurtful insults.

Olga Ivinskaya was Boris Pasternak's lover for fourteen years. They became acquainted, she says, in 1947, in the offices of *Noviy Mir*, where she worked as an editor and Pasternak would call to deal with tedious matters of publication. She was beautiful, with typically Muscovite fair hair, aged thirty, a poet. He was famous, but dubious and problematic, nearing sixty. So far, the clichés look familiar. Later events blow them away like a storm.

The story starts with the poet's wife, usually portrayed as the loser in this duel. With some hesitation, the 'interpreters' of *Doctor Zhivago* point out that the rivalry between Olga Ivinskaya and Pasternak's wife was a highly charged one. First, Zinaida Pasternak was in no way a loser. Many recall the memorable concert given by her first husband, the pianist Heinrich Neuhaus, who suddenly burst into tears and let his head fall on to the piano because he had found out that his wife was flirting with Pasternak.

Later, the idea spread that men in the 1920s and 1930s cried more readily than those of subsequent years, but collapsing in tears in front of an audience of 300 because your wife is leaving you is an undeniably rare occurrence.

This Bach-style confession, if that is what striking your forehead against the piano can be called, would in itself have made Zinaida Neuhaus a focus for romantic attention. What a striking story it became, when it was discovered who had lost his wife, and to whom.

The poet was not only aware of this incident, but was in the auditorium when it took place. Moreover, he, the victorious rival, did exactly the same as the man he had defeated, and burst into tears.

Boris Pasternak did marry Zinaida Neuhaus, but there were still further surprises in his love life. The most shocking was no doubt the events of 1949 when, just as his idyll with Olga Ivins-kaya was at its most perfect, the dark shadow of prison fell between them.

In such cases one's first assumption is that the husband is under threat, especially when he is under a heavy cloud of suspicion, as Pasternak was. However, it wasn't him but his sweet fair-haired lover who landed in handcuffs.

This may have seemed shocking at first, but wasn't in fact all that unexpected. In such cases, despite who was put in handcuffs, it was the man who was the principal target. Not for the first or last time, a beautiful woman found herself confronted with horror.

In this case, there was another cliché rumoured, a more subtle one than usual, about how a beautiful woman would extract information from Pasternak where the Bobrovs, Surkovs, Duvak-ins, the five S. sisters and Zhdanov's closing speech had failed.

If this proved unnecessary because the poet's

gloomy temperament was well known, then another reason remained: to put pressure on the writer by imprisoning his lover. Hostage-taking is as old as the world. Meanwhile, Olga was pregnant by Pasternak, which made her imprisonment doubly significant.

Other speculation of the most incredible kind still blossomed everywhere. Was Olga Ivinskaya just a flirtatious Muscovite or an agent of the CIA, of the sort being exposed more and more often? Or worse, was she a double agent? Was Olga in spite of all appearances herself a woman of importance – not put in place to inform on Pasternak, but the other way round, with Pasternak placed to inform on her?

The confusion deepened. Nobody understood what people were saying, not to mention what they thought, or the meaning of the events themselves. 'Don't you understand anything?' the theatre director Meyerhold had asked, half joking. And had added: to understand it, read *Macbeth*.

Everybody began to think more often of the theatre. Theatre, terror, terrified. In most European languages, the word 'terror' sounds close. In the whispering about Pasternak, sometimes malicious but sometimes in quiet admiration, people mentioned the translation of *Hamlet* that he'd been working on for years.

Hamlet, whether the play or the character, is an act of detachment from its times. The alliance between the Danish prince and the ghost emphasises this detachment.

This exteriorisation implies a question of who is to blame, the individual or his times? It is of course easier to believe in the fault of an individual or individuals, not to say entire peoples, than the guilt of an entire age.

A closer look at the Pasternak–Hamlet resemblance reveals the complication of the father–son relationship. Hamlet finds out from the ghost the truth about the murder of his father the king. In the relationship between Boris Pasternak and the Soviet state, there was also a murder, that of the child that Olga Ivinskaya was carrying when she went to prison. The story was comparable, with the murder of a son instead of a father, but critics of the time were attracted less by the resemblance to *Hamlet* than by the relationship with Goethe's *Faust*, also translated by Pasternak. In *Faust*, besides an imprisoned lover, Margarete, who recalls Ivinskaya, there is also something more devious and mysterious: a pact with the devil. And we know that in the communist world, whenever distinguished writers were concerned, this kind of pact was always in people's minds, even if they spoke of it less.

Meanwhile, Russian life found its own solution. Events took their course, and after their fourteen-year adventure, full of unexpected drama (Ivinskaya would be imprisoned once again, together with her daughter), the graves of the two, Boris and Olga, would lie next to one another in Peredelkino.

Where they are to this day, as I write these lines.

ELEVENTH VERSION

The hope for an account as impartial as possible rests on the testimony of someone who was actually a distant figure: the distinguished British philosopher, historian and diplomat Isaiah Berlin.

One sleepless night spent with a Russian woman was enough to split Isaiah Berlin's life story into two parts, one ordinary and British, and the other extraordinary and Russo-Soviet.

Anyone who thinks this exaggerated will change their mind on learning the name of the woman: Anna Andreyevna Gorenko, otherwise Anna Akhmatova.

This night really happened, in November 1945, in a genuinely Russian and at the same time Soviet city, St Petersburg, alias Leningrad. A sleepless night in the apartment of the famous poet. Just as Stalin really uttered the words, 'So our sister is bringing foreign spies home.'

Anna Gorenko was seemingly dogged by disaster, from the shooting of her first husband Nikolai Gumilev in 1921, when he was just twenty years old, down to Zhdanov's public description of her at the age of fifty as 'half nun, half whore'.

Her second husband, Nikolai Punin, ended up in prison in 1938, and if that were not enough her only son Lev Gumilev was arrested in the same year. One can imagine the nightmare, the endless worry, the waiting for visits at the prison door, not to mention the suspicion, the publication ban, the loneliness and the venomous criticism.

This would be a burden for anybody, but especially for a woman and even a diva, who paid in advance for her future fame, her reception in Oxford and her belated world triumph. But neither her dreamlike debut, in love with one of the most famous Russian poets, drawn by Amedeo

Modigliani, one of the world's artistic geniuses, in a café in Montparnasse, nor her protracted farewell, when books, poems, memoirs and even musical plays would portray her, could do anything to compensate for her grief.

To go back to Pasternak, Mandelstam and that sleepless night. There is some truth in Akhmatova's apparently naive remark that the East–West Cold War began on that same November night. People's perception of that cold night, at the time or later or even today, is probably not far from Stalin's, i.e. erotic. This is a complication, a trap, a dark region, that nobody is certain about, but which occurs to everybody. There is no certainty about this. There are Akhmatova's own poems and remarks, and Berlin's statements. The British visitor never forgot that night. He was young and lived for fifty years after it. He died in 1997, when Anna, if she had lived on, would have been 107.

Immediately after the 'St Anna's night' that

changed his life, Isaiah Berlin rushed to Moscow to meet Pasternak. It was 1945, and Berlin sensed that he would be expelled from the Soviet Union, as indeed happened the following year.

So he had reason to hurry and not forget anything. The memorable night with Anna was deepened by her wide-ranging conversation, part of which was conditioned by the to-and-fro of the Moscow–St Petersburg rail service, which Akhmatova generally took with her inseparable friend Lydia Chukovskaya, the daughter of Korney Chukovsky. Muffled by train whistles and the clicking of the rails, they would discuss all recent events, from the possible arrival of Rainer Maria Rilke from Vienna to the plausible role of the French in the suicide of Mayakovsky, through Lilya Brik's sister. It would be hard to keep Pasternak out of this imbroglio. In fact the British writer's dash to Moscow immediately after leaving St Anna suggests that Pasternak featured in their interminable conversation.

'I can talk about this story as I remember it from what Pasternak himself told me in 1945,' writes Berlin. 'According to Pasternak, only he himself and his wife and son were present when the phone rang in the communal apartment on Volkonskaya Street in Moscow.'

Isaiah Berlin told this story several times.

According to Pasternak, after an introduction familiar from more or less all the versions, an unknown voice came on the phone. The poet imagined that someone was playing a joke on him, but Stalin explained that it really was himself, and went on to ask if Pasternak had been present when Mandelstam had read his squib in verse. Pasternak replied that it didn't seem important to him whether he'd been present or not and that he was happy to be talking to Stalin. He had always known that this would happen and they should meet to discuss some matters of extraordinary importance. Stalin asked whether Mandelstam was a fine poet. Pasternak replied that as poets they were entirely different and that he valued Mandelstam's poems. He didn't feel an inner rapport with Mandelstam, but this wasn't the point.

As he related this episode, Pasternak plunged into metaphysical views about turning points in history, about which he wanted to talk to Stalin in a deep conversation of historic significance. Ignoring this, Stalin asked him once more if he'd been present or not when Mandelstam recited his verses. Pasternak answered that the most important thing was for him to meet with Stalin, that this meeting mustn't be put off, and everything depended on it, in that they had to talk about the most important things, life and death.

'If I were Mandelstam's friend, I would

know how to defend him better,' said Stalin, and hung up.

Pasternak tried to phone back, but without success. This entire story seemed to cause him great pain. This is how he told it to me, as outlined here, on at least two occasions.

(Isaiah Berlin, *Meetings with Russian Writers*, Moscow, 2011.)

The British visitor says that he heard the story of the phone call from Pasternak himself, twice. This shows that there is no question of anything unclear about the events.

There are some questions. Did the phone call really take place? If it did, could it be reproduced exactly? And finally, did this British guest fully understand the Russian poet's account?

This question arises especially in relation to the final part of the story, the return call that didn't happen. Or couldn't happen.

Pasternak's generally confused speech seems to have made this fog thicker.

There is the question of the poet's attempt to call Stalin again. The secretary's curt reply showed there would be no second phone call.

That is the long and short of it.

Pasternak perhaps felt that he hadn't properly understood Stalin. Perhaps the thought of who he was talking to prevented him from concentrating.

The strange thing is that the misunderstanding persisted even after the secretary had stopped speaking, when the poet was trying to recall everything calmly. Indeed the secretary's words seemed more and more elusive.

He felt that they would always remain so and that they could never be replaced by ordinary phrases of refusal, such as: Comrade Stalin regrets, but he is very busy. Or: don't disturb Comrade Stalin. Or worse: what was to be said has been said. If not: Comrade Stalin does not wish to speak to you further.

Sometimes Pasternak interspersed his own speech with traces of these phrases, which the secretary never uttered.

At other times he reproached himself for worrying more than he should. He was a great writer and shouldn't rack his brains to discover what was going on in someone else's mind, even in the Kremlin itself. On the contrary, he himself was part of the world's mystery – so let other people analyse him if they were so keen.

Recently, for instance, there had been renewed rumours that Anna Akhmatova had claimed to have written some of her verses while she was dead.

When Pasternak heard this, he had taken it for a manner of speaking, the sort of thing associated with Anna. Later it seemed more and more natural in the context of the bright light that the art of socialist realism was supposed to spread, in contrast to the murk of decadence.

This light was encouraged at endless meetings

and plenums. People came to understand how pitiful was the absence of light in art. They could even imagine the compassion that Homer aroused in the ladies who passed by, stopping to listen to him on the street corner. How beautifully that bard sings! What a sin that he has no eyes. They could say what miracles he would work, if only he had them.

It would require maybe centuries to think of his mocking riposte: they're making light of the gods' greatest gift to me: the loss of my eyes. The gods knew that I had no need of eyes, and might even find them a hindrance.

So people spoke of his blindness, unable to decide whether it was a punishment or a gift. Then it was no longer mentioned, just as there was never any mention of the human being closest to him, the poet's wife, Mrs Homer. She it most certainly was who eased the titanic labours of this lord of art. For example, she probably wrote down his second poem *The Odyssey*, if the master had left it incomplete.

Which of her poems had Anna written while she was dead, as she put it? And why had she insisted that this was what she had done?

It might be an example of what the plenums deplored as 'intentional obfuscation' or perhaps it was something deeper. This phrase contained an outright threat. In the lecture halls of the Gorky Institute the first-year students were not alone in believing that Sholokhov had done great harm with his perpetual optimism. Apparently the author himself had tried to moderate his enthusiasm. It was as if distorting spectacles damaged your eyes.

People were right to shake their heads in incomprehension. This bright, broad Soviet homeland, as it was put. Full of placards, pioneers and rallies. And yet awash with mysteries, where they were least expected.

What were these eyes whose sight had to be dimmed? These phone calls that came once in a lifetime? These Sholokhovs with a third eye . . . or these Annas, who wrote when they were dead?

What was going on? Shouldn't there be a cry of 'Enough!' to all this? And some other explanation?

Of course there should.

TWELFTH VERSION

What was going on?

The tyrant was having fun . . .

These are the words of Vladimir Solovyev, a specialist writing about these times and author of the book *The Ghost That Eats Its Own Elbows*. The author was also suspected of being a KGB agent, and admitted as much in 1992.

It would be hard to utter more venomous

words against poets. Behind them lies a sick envy of artists and a sinister worship of the tyrants who oppress them. Above all, there is a covert desire that this should be true, that the tyrant was having fun.

The whole notion is malicious and perverse, because the entire mentality of oppression from which it springs is perverse.

The tyrant and the poet, however much they may seem opposites, both held *power*. The first associations of the word *power* can only be grim: oppression, violence, dispossession. Yet human language has also thought of gentler usages. Power can be used for bad ends, but an artistic genius has power, and so does a sweet fair-haired woman.

In this context, a precise meaning must be sought for that treacherous phrase, 'the tyrant was having fun'. Was he having fun with the poet? Looking for further definition, we might ask if the tyrant was capable of having fun at all.

Could the tyrant bring the poet to his knees? Could he overthrow him? The same question might be asked of the poet, confronted with the tyrant.

This dualistic history is built upon a pair of opposites: enthronement and dethronement. Though they may seem distant these two are close. Two or three poets might share one throne, something that has never happened with tyrants. The throne in art might be left vacant for several centuries, but that doesn't happen with tyrants. For them, the moment of dethronement comes as a surprise. For a king, or more precisely a kingdom, it happens in an instant, with a knife blow or a few drops of poison, but sometimes for a poet a thousand years aren't enough.

This comparison of poets and tyrants may seem implausible, yet one's obsession with it grows. It is devious, ambiguous and dangerous, but maybe for those reasons all the more tempting.

To go back to the conversation with Stalin: this phone call in a void, instead of fading into oblivion as time has passed, looms ever larger in the memory.

Pasternak started with an attempt to forget it. (To hell with it, why should he and not Stalin rake over the details of this conversation?) There was the obscurity of what the secretary said, and everything else. There was indeed a kind of fog, but perhaps not as much as at first there seemed. After all, Pasternak had spoken with a mere secretary, not with Plato. And he had no reason to pay attention to Stalin's gentler words, if that is what they were.

So he thought, but this didn't stop him from changing his mind a short time later. What harm was there in recollecting the details? As we know, unexpected things come from these details. Also, it was a conversation about fundamental matters, especially the fate of Mandelstam.

It was the kind of event that didn't happen every day. He and Stalin had spoken for a few moments on the phone and might never speak again. One of the two speakers then didn't pick up the receiver, and yet they were both still alive, Pasternak of course, and Stalin, God help him, the same. What had died was the telephone.

Pasternak had stretched out his hand to the receiver, uncertain whether he wanted to pick it up in good faith or throw it down. His hand remained frozen in the air and at that moment the apparatus gave a muffled signal.

Then came the voice of the secretary from the Kremlin.

'What?' Pasternak had asked, while the other man said something truly startling.

Pasternak imagined uttering a second 'what', even more unnecessary than the first.

The remainder of his words, however few, were even more useless.

Pasternak thought that he had managed to say the word 'misunderstanding' before he repeated his request to speak with Stalin once more.

The reply had come abruptly down the wire. 'Comrade Stalin doesn't, Comrade St— . . . Comrade St— hadn't . . . perhaps something . . . perhaps another time. Comrade St— simply did not wish . . .'

It was all these phrases together or maybe none of them.

Of course none of them. Nevertheless among these fragments Pasternak thought that he'd heard something incredible.

It was beyond incredible, to the point where whenever he recalled it there arose a suspicion that it could be a fiction of his mind.

In his exhausted state, he mentally rehearsed everything, until, not without regret, he was sure that it was all true.

What was incredible came from a gentler form

of understanding that reached him from a distance, even though it did not offer any redress for the cruel disdain with which the poet's request for an explanation had been rejected, but banished any hope of such a thing.

Comrade Stalin ... no. Comrade St—. Doesn't. Com. St. Never ...

According to the secretary, that telephone line, unlike any other in the world, had been created for a single use, for one conversation. For the conversation that had just been conducted ... Immediately afterwards, in a manner nobody could know, the line had vanished.

He had never heard of anything crazier.

The question of how a telephone line could cease to exist haunted him. Was it to do with the wire, or something else that the mind couldn't grasp? Perhaps it came from the kingdom of death, that desolate landscape which he thought he knew better than others.

In essence, this was doubtless the case, it came

from the utmost depths where there were still no words for such complicated matters, such as that lack of any meeting between the poet and the tyrant.

He knew something of this landscape of course, but nothing so pitiless as what had reached him through this commonplace instrument used by millions of human hands and which had suddenly become filled with mystery.

It was probable that all Moscow had heard the whispered rumour. Pasternak had wanted to talk to the big chief, but nature itself had obstructed it.

Worn out with speculation, people would come to believe that, among other mysteries, a telephone had been destined to appear that self-destructed after a single conversation.

History is usually reticent regarding what happens between poets and tyrants. The truth gives way to inventions, some memorable, others forgettable.

Two madmen lived in Rome
One Seneca, and one Nero.

According to an ancient death ritual, this dramatist of genius spent most of his time from morning
to night in the emperor's court.

All Rome talked of them and was unable to
decide who was having the most fun. At first
sight, the answer would obviously be the emperor,
especially when in the last episode of the chroni-
cle Seneca lies in his bath, cutting his veins on
the emperor's order.

So the scene was clear: Rome's foremost poet in
the warm bath, trying to ease his passage to death
with the help of carefully cut veins and warm
water. Not far off, the tyrant of Rome waited with
curiosity for news of his progress towards death.
Dozens of chroniclers and spies hurried from one
to the other with the latest information, the blood
was flowing faster or slower, the water was cool-
ing, there might be hope of a pardon.

Meanwhile Rome seethed with news and rumours. The chronicles, strangely, never express any sympathy for the dramatist. Instead of describing the nightmare experienced by the poor poet, their interpretation is that the poet and the tyrant were mortal enemies.

Seneca had long been the focus of rumours. As if the benefits of the imperial palace were not enough, he made love to the tyrant's mother, who was also the aunt of the future king. By all accounts, Nero was aware of this, but their 'estrangement' had nothing to do with it. Indeed, Nero had later murdered his own mother, though not for this reason, and for Seneca and Nero this episode was over and done with. Meanwhile, the reason for the 'estrangement', while unimportant itself, like most tyrants' impulses, reminds us that human memory, even when not defamatory, has not treated great poets with tenderness.

This is most nakedly evident in the cliché that

poets need no defence. Both parties know this, humanity and the poets.

The expression 'Russia today has two tsars', that is the tsar and Tolstoy, the country's most famous writer, was the kind of phrase that seemed to rise to the lofty spheres of poetry, celestial regions and kings, yet it spread through all countries and times, and earned everybody's slight contempt. What did people make of the expression?

The saying was received in two ways. The great mass of readers would probably have chosen the writer over the tsar. But what of the rivals themselves, the writer and the tsar? Of them, it might be said that, instead of being touched by the popularity, they were both annoyed, the writer most of all, and the tsar less.

Russia couldn't have two tsars any more than it could have two suns or two moons. But an incomparable miracle had taken place, that the tsar could acquire a double in a man without a crown or a throne, or any kind of royal connection.

So curiosity focuses principally on their rivalry.

The Russian tsar of the time was called Romanov. There is no evidence of his opinion of Tolstoy, and still less of any comparison with him (such as 'Russia today has two Tolstoys').

Meanwhile Tolstoy, to his misfortune and our own great regret, gave his tongue free rein and left nothing unsaid against the tsar. His insults are surprisingly vulgar and unworthy of a grey-haired Russian genius.

'Russia has two tsars' . . . the treason in the expression is obvious. Russia, like every mon-archy, could only have one tsar, and this notion of a double monarch can be interpreted in favour of the challenger.

The expression doesn't in any way resonate to the writer's discredit. (Russia has a tsar, why does it need another? for example.) In its endless rep-etition, it affirms only admiration for the genius of literature. (We thought we had a proper tsar, before we knew anything about this other one . . . the real one.)

As time passed, the progress of this strange story, or the desire to bring it to an end, would probably have ended in the question of whether the great Tolstoy could have behaved like this.

The answer must lie between two possible exclamations. Of course not! Or, of course, why not?

Leo Tolstoy was not a reticent man. His conversations at Yasnaya Polyana, although often of a delicate nature, like those with Chekhov and Gorky, were famous. It is enough to look at these to banish any false sense of mystery.

At first sight, one's impression is that Tolstoy never mentions the Russian tsar, and must have been one of the few people ignorant of the famous saying about the double thrones.

Tolstoy does talk about a monarch of literature, but this is not a tsar or a Russian. He is a distant Englishman, of whose good name Tolstoy is careless, William Shakespeare. And to avoid any misunderstanding, or the idea this is another Shakespeare and not the one we know, he goes on to mention *Hamlet* and *Macbeth* as two of the most useless texts of this worthless writer.

It is hard to credit.

How insignificant this tsar now appears beside the majesty of the writer-tsar.

Shakespeare has to be toppled.

He's not only not great, but less than mediocre.

What is this appalling blindness?

In the family of geniuses, there are occasionally signs of envy, but nothing like this.

Was this a moment of anger? A loss of balance? Maybe, or a fit of madness?

No, there are thousands of examples in Tolstoy's interminable conversations, with serious people. Russia and not just Russia, but the whole world including England, the country that gave him birth, must bring down Shakespeare!

THIRTEENTH VERSION

Epilogue

Rarely has so much been said and written about a phone conversation. Analysts have pored over the records endlessly and insisted on conflicting opinions. Archive sources have not helped to establish a reliable version of the conversation and have even prompted suspicions that it never happened at all.

In fact the phone call did take place. It was Saturday, 23 June 1934. The names of the two participants have been established: Yosif Stalin, the supreme leader of a most dangerous state, and Boris Pasternak, the distinguished writer, unloved by this state and its leader.

The archives also give the length of the conversation as between three and four minutes. All the words said by each participant are clearly evidenced and preserved. The two speakers state where they are located, one in the Kremlin and the other in the writer's Moscow apartment.

At first sight there is nothing unclear, not to say 'mysterious', about this conversation. One of the speakers, Stalin, asks questions of the other, Pasternak, about a third writer whose name is on everybody's lips because of his arrest, Osip Mandelstam.

Pasternak gives answers of a sort, but the chief is not satisfied with his replies, to the point that he hangs up the phone.

The conversation becomes more complicated because it enters another dimension, what might be called 'the zone of death'. It is this that brings about the misunderstandings and the mystery that will persist for decades.

Belonging simultaneously as it does to two mutually exclusive dimensions, the incident impresses upon us its impossibility. It strikes an alarm bell that will not let any human conscience rest easy. Osip Mandelstam wasn't and won't be alone in his remote exile. And this is why we find it easier and more natural, avoiding the grandiose word 'immortal', to say that Mandelstam and those like him are 'without end'.

ISMAIL KADARE is Albania's best-known novelist and poet. Translations of his novels have appeared in more than forty countries. He was awarded the inaugural Man Booker International Prize in 2005, the Jerusalem Prize in 2015, and the Neustadt International Prize for Literature in 2020.

JOHN HODGSON studied at Cambridge and Newcastle and has taught at the universities of Prishtina and Tirana. This is the seventeenth book by Ismail Kadare that he has translated.